VLADIVOSTOK
CIRCUS

Also by Elisa Shua Dusapin

Winter in Sokcho
The Pachinko Parlour

VLADIVOSTOK CIRCUS

ELISA SHUA DUSAPIN

TRANSLATED BY ANEESA ABBAS HIGGINS

This edition first published in the United Kingdom in 2024 by
Daunt Books Originals
83 Marylebone High Street
London W1U 4QW

1

Copyright © Éditions Zoé, 2022

English translation copyright © 2024 Aneesa Abbas Higgins
With the support of the Swiss Arts Council Pro Helvetia

First published in 2022 by Éditions Zoé, France

A CIP catalogue record for this title
is available from the British Library.

ISBN 978-1-914198-31-1

Typeset by Marsha Swan

Printed and bound by TJ Books Ltd, Padstow, Cornwall

www.dauntbookspublishing.co.uk

PART I

THEY DON'T SEEM to be expecting me. The man in the ticket booth checks the list of names for the hundredth time. He's just ushered out a group of women, all with the same muscular build, their hair scraped back. I can see the glass dome of the building on the other side of the barrier, the marbled stone of the walls beneath this season's posters. I'm here for the costumes, I tell him again. In the end he turns away, stares at a television screen. He probably doesn't understand English, I think to myself. I sit down on my suitcase, try calling Leon, the director, the one I've been corresponding with. My phone battery flashes low: only 3 per cent left. I hear myself laugh nervously as I look around for somewhere to charge it. I'm about to walk away when I hear someone calling out to me from inside the circus building. A man comes running towards me, steadying his glasses on his nose. Tall and lanky, not at all like the girls I saw a moment ago. I'd say he was in his thirties.

'Sorry,' he says in English. 'I wasn't expecting you until next week! I'm Leon.'

'Beginning of November. Isn't that what we said?'

'You're right, I'm all over the place.'

He leads me round the outside of the building to a small courtyard, fenced on one side. Beyond the fence, the ocean, the shoreline visible through the gaps. Paper lanterns dangle from the branches of a tree. A beige-coloured caravan looms large over the metal furniture set out beside it. Tables littered with plates, some doubling as ashtrays, others streaked with tomato sauce. Scrunched-up sportswear and lace-trimmed undergarments strewn on chairs.

I follow him inside the building, down a dark, curving hallway. He translates the signs pinned to the doors for me: offices, backstage access, arena floor. Bedrooms and dressing rooms upstairs. We come to a staircase. He excuses himself for a moment saying he needs to catch the circus director at dinner and runs up the stairs.

A cat gazes at me from the top of the staircase, its coat is white, almost pink. I stretch out my hand and the cat pads down the stairs towards me. The peculiar pinkish hue is its skin colour. A cat with almost no fur. It rubs up against my legs. I pull myself upright, feeling vaguely repulsed.

Leon comes back, another man at his side, fiftyish, platinum-coloured hair, firm handshake. He starts talking to me in Russian; Leon translates for me as he speaks. He's sorry about the misunderstanding, I'm a bit early. A short laugh. He's certainly not going to turn me away, I've come such a great distance. He's honoured to be hosting a talented young designer from the European fashion world. Vladivostok Circus's major autumn show is still running. It'll be closing for the winter at the end of the week. Until then, I'm welcome to come to as many shows as I like. The only problem is accommodation: the rooms are all taken by the artists. I can move in after they've left.

I force a smile, say I'll manage just fine. The director claps his hands, perfect! I mustn't hesitate to ask him if there's anything I need.

He disappears into his office before I have a chance to respond. I thank Leon for translating. He shrugs. He used to teach English, he's Canadian. He's happy to help me. I tell him what's on my mind: I've only just finished college, my training's been in theatre and film, I've never worked for a circus, he did know that, didn't he? And I'm not sure I understand how this is all going to work if the artists are all leaving at the end of the season. Leon nods. Yes, it wasn't really made clear. Usually, everyone leaves, the performers all go and work for Christmas circuses. But our group, the Russian bar trio, have arranged with the director to stay on here at the circus rent-free while they work on their new number. They'll perform it at the Vladivostok spring show in exchange.

'Anton and Nino are big stars,' Leon explains. 'It's a good deal for the circus. Not sure if it's so good for Anton and Nino, but that's the way it is.'

I try and look convinced, sizing up the gulf that separates me from this world. All I know about the three I'm working with is that they're famous for their Black Bird number, in which Igor, the flyer, performs five perilous triple jumps on the Russian bar. I've looked it up and gleaned some information about this piece of equipment: it's a flexible bar, three metres in length with a diameter of twenty centimetres. The two bases carry the bar on their shoulders while the third member of the group executes moves on it, leaping high in the air and flying free, without a wire. It's one of the most dangerous of all circus acts.

'Were you the one who created the number with Igor?' I ask.

'No, not me. I didn't even know him before his accident.'

'Accident?'

'Didn't you know? He hasn't jumped for five years. They have a new flyer. Anna.'

He says she's gone into town with Nino, but Anton's here, in his room. He can introduce me if I like, or else tomorrow after the show. I tell him tomorrow will be fine.

'Yes, that's probably best. Anton can get by in quite a few languages but he doesn't speak much English.'

The show has finished for today. He has to tidy up. Would I like to come with him? I'm very tired, I say, I have to find a hotel, and what about my luggage? Oh, he'll help me with all that, he says, with a sweeping gesture of the hand.

Backstage a pungent animal smell hits me. Straw scattered on the ground. Streaks of dirt on the walls. Like a stable but with velvet lining – hoops instead of horses, waist-high wooden balls, metal poles, tangles of cables, drones in the shape of planes, straw hats hanging on hooks. Leon tugs a cord and the curtains part.

I walk out into the ring. Carpeting on the ground, rumpled here and there, talcum powder and splashes of water, traces of the show that finished earlier. The space seems smaller than I'd expected, less imposing than when seen from the outside. Four hundred seats at the most. Red risers, velvet-covered seating. A platform overhangs the public entrance, with six chairs, music stands, a drum set and a double bass.

'Do you need a hand?' I ask, watching Leon climb up one of the towers located at intervals around the edge of the ring.

He doesn't respond and I breathe a sigh of relief. I can't see myself going up there to join him. He unhooks a trapeze, disturbing one of the spotlight projectors as he moves around. The spotlight begins to wobble, its beam falling on a torn curtain over a window. I can see a section of the sky through the tear in the fabric. It's dark outside, and still only six o'clock. The sky is studded with stars.

Leon starts rolling up a carpet.

'Can I do anything to help?' I say again.

He shakes his head, straining from the effort. With the dirt floor freed from its covering, the odour intensifies, as if the smell emanated from here, from unseen animals trampled beneath our feet.

'It smells pretty strong.'

'It stinks, you mean!' Leon exclaims.

He says the circus doesn't use animals now. He hasn't seen any in the seven years he's been working here. The smell hasn't gone away though. No one seems to know why.

'It's not so bad right now, but in the summer, with the heat, the lights, the people, it really stinks.'

He glances around the ring and adds in a hushed voice: 'I don't think any of this has ever been properly cleaned.'

He goes backstage again. The lights go down. I turn back to look at the ring again before joining him. A gleam of light from a lamppost filters in through a gap in the curtains, casting a yellow glow on the risers. It makes everything look much more old-fashioned, a scene from another century. The beam of light hits the double bass. Lying on its side, the bow across its hips, the bass looks as if it's resting, weary of carving out its tune, waiting for tomorrow's performance.

LEON HAS FOUND me a hotel in the centre of town, two kilometres from the circus, opposite the port and the station. A Soviet-era building, corridors that go on for ever, enormous rooms, salmon-coloured walls adorned with still-life prints. I came up the emergency stairs so I'd know the way if the lift breaks down. From the window, I can see the ferries for Japan, China and Korea coming and going, trains heading to St Petersburg and Moscow, nine thousand kilometres west of here, a six-day journey.

I unpack my suitcase, fold my clothes. I don't have much, my winter boots, warm jumper and corduroy dungarees take up most of the space. I double-check my supply of tools: needles, scissor case, glue, paint, make-up, scraps of fabric, thread and my lightweight portable sewing machine, which I leave in its case. There's no table in here for me to set it up. Annoyingly, there's no fridge either, despite what the website says and I'll be staying here for quite a while. Still, I'd rather be here than at the circus. The idea of living in such close proximity to people I don't know doesn't appeal to me.

In the shower, I inspect the patch of psoriasis on the back of my neck. It started when I handed in my project for my diploma at the beginning of the summer. I'm sure it's spreading. I flop backwards onto the bed, not bothering to dry my hair, and watch videos about Russian bar. The bases cross their forearms over the bar, body tensed, leaning forward, head turned up towards the flyer. The picture on my phone is fuzzy, the connection slow. It makes their movements seem jerky, they look like humanoid insects. I google Anna, the flyer. The Vladivostok Circus website says she's from Ukraine. She was a trampoline champion before making a name for herself in Russian bar. She's one of only three female athletes able to perform four perilous triple jumps. She's twenty-two, the same age as me.

I close the screen, a catch in my throat. The next few months suddenly seem like an eternity.

THE ANIMAL STENCH has gone, replaced by a smell of sugar. I'm sitting in the back row, my view of the ring obstructed by one of the towers. If I lean to the right, I can see a little more. I did have a better seat but I offered it to a child. His mother wanted him to give me his popcorn to say thank you, but the little boy started yelling so I said there was no need.

The orchestra strikes up a chord and the parade begins. I count about thirty performers. The costumes draw mostly on Russian and Chinese traditions, with some inspired by western European medieval dress – royalty, religion. Harlequin-style designs for the clowns.

A bit clichéd in my opinion. Juggling acts, contortionists, strongmen. The Asian girls form human pyramids on the waist-high balls I saw backstage. The youngest one standing on someone's shoulders can't be more than twelve years old. She topples over several times and is caught just in time by the girls on the ground. Even when she falls, her fixed smile never wavers. Behind them is the trapeze artist, hanging by his teeth as he performs circles in the air, arms and legs spread wide.

I wait expectantly for the Russian bar act.

At the interval the audience crowd around the snack bars. I avoid them and stand in the corridor. The curve of the wall is disorienting. I start walking around, working out where I am from the dates on the posters on the walls. They are displayed in chronological order, starting with 1919, a freak show: dwarves, a bearded lady, Hercules the strongman, a fire eater. Lots of animals: bears, tigers, elephants. Mid-century: horses bedecked in finery, red-nosed clowns. Oriental dancers in 1987. Vacant smiles. All of them wreathed in smoke, like cheerful zombies, floating weightlessly. And then I'm back where I started, with the high-tech drones of the 21st century, the colours as muted as in the 1919 poster. I realise the fading is not the work of time but the artist's intention. The posters must all have been made quite recently.

The second half begins with the Russian bar act. I recognise the bases from the videos I watched on my phone. Anton and Nino. They come on dressed as corsairs. Anna in a ripped dress. A woman held captive, trying to break free. The choreography alternates between routines on the bar and choreographed steps on firm ground. They are out of time with the orchestra – I can't tell if the music is getting faster of if they are falling behind the beat. Anna seems to be rushing her steps to keep up with the tempo. I find it unnerving. Each time she takes flight I lean in as she rises through the air and hangs, suspended for an instant, before falling back down and bounding up again, higher and higher every time. She reaches a height of six or seven metres. Finally, the orchestra falls silent. The trio bow. Applause. Anna climbs back onto the bar. Solo drum roll. The bases adjust their hold. Anna raises her arms, tilts her chin defiantly and performs one final perilous leap. It ends with a full twist. Another round of applause, louder than before. She must have added one more spin, I didn't manage to count. Once their performance is over I have trouble concentrating on the other acts. But the trio might want me to tell them later what I think of theirs so I stay to the very end of the show.

OUTSIDE I MEET UP with Leon and the two bases, who are still in their costumes but without their make-up. The younger one is closer to my age, a little older perhaps. He towers over me, he must be at least eleven inches taller than I am. He has angelic curls that seem out of place with his powerful build. He grins at me and says:

'It's so great that you're here. I'm Nino. And this is Anton.'

The other one is stockier, barrel-chested, he looks old enough to be Nino's father. He smiles wistfully at me, eyebrows rising and forehead crinkling. I compliment them on their act and his expression deepens.

'Anna's resting at the moment,' Nino says. 'She's going to join us this evening. She'll be so happy to meet you.'

He turns to Anton, who doesn't react.

'Okay,' says Leon. 'I'm off to put things away. I'll see you in the canteen!'

I watch as he disappears from view, butterflies in my stomach.

The canteen rings with the clatter of cutlery. Metal tables, green-tiled floor. In the glare of the neon lights, the domed ceiling looks like a giant birdcage. We queue up with the performers. The food on their trays is almost all in varying shades of white. There's something liquid – a kind of béchamel sauce; some sort of grain – rice or cracked wheat perhaps; and something smooth that looks like puréed mashed potatoes. Beer seems to be the favourite drink.

'Hungry?' asks Anton, patting his stomach.

We're served by a plump, mournful-looking young woman. I opt for something that looks like macaroni cheese, with a beer. Nino sighs as he pours himself a glass of fruit juice; he's banned himself from drinking when he's working. Anton gave up alcohol a long time ago. I put my beer back, mumbling something incoherent. I never drink beer. I don't even like it. I was trying to look relaxed.

We sit down at a table away from the counter. I ask them about their daily routine here. This is their first stay in Vladivostok. They've been here for two months. Two weeks of rehearsal, six weeks of shows, two performances a day, Wednesday to Sunday. I'm surprised at the number of performances.

'We often have a full house,' says Nino. 'Vladivostok Circus is huge. It's the biggest in the region.'

All the same, I have a hard time imagining so many people coming to the circus. Nino goes on talking. On working days they get up at eight and have breakfast, then rehearse in the ring, half an hour on each number. After that they wait, warm up, do their first show, have a light meal, then more waiting, warming up again, a second show, a meal and then rest.

'That's all the training you do?'

'It's just to keep the act sharp. We make small corrections, adjust a few details for the next show. Two sessions a day is already quite a lot. Any more would be too much. The real work will happen later this autumn, with you.'

He explains that they're preparing for an international circus festival that's being held a thousand miles to the west in Ulan-Ude just before Christmas. It's a big event, one of the biggest, and it's just over six weeks away. He and Anton have won prizes there before but this will be the first time they've entered a competition with Anna.

'How long have you been working together?' I ask.

'With Anna, one year.'

He glances over at Anton:

'With him, nineteen.'

Nino laughs at my puzzled expression.

'I was eight when he took me on.'

Anton mutters something into his food. Nino laughs again, harder:

'He knows it was child exploitation. You can't get away with that sort of thing these days. But if it weren't for him, I wouldn't be here at all. He says it's no wonder standards among children have dropped. No one dares train them anymore. But things are different in Russia. Luckily for us.'

Anton is Buryat, from the Lake Baikal region. Nino is German. His parents ran a circus in Bremen. They enrolled him in the Moscow circus school when he was seven. They'd heard that Anton was starting to train young people there. Anton was famous. He'd had a long career performing with his wife and was getting ready to retire. Nino was one of his first pupils. They developed an acrobatic routine together, with lifts that showcased Anton's great strength, and started touring with it. At first it was only with Nino's parents' circus but they soon started attracting attention. Nino was given funding and left school to train and perform full time. By the time he was fourteen he was becoming too heavy for Anton to lift but the rapport they'd developed made it easy for them to move into Russian bar. And Igor, who was just a little younger than Nino, was their flyer.

'That's when things really started to happen for us,' Nino explains. 'The US, Canada, Europe, Russia, China. We went everywhere.'

Anton stands up abruptly and says the food's tasteless, he's going to get some pickles. Nino gives me an apologetic look:

'Not much of a restaurant, is it? Sorry about that.'

I tell him it doesn't bother me, it takes me back to my childhood. I lived here when I was little.

'You did?'

'Yes, just after the town was opened to foreigners. My father had a research post at the university.'

Leon arrives, followed by Anna dressed in a velour tracksuit, her cheeks flushed. She looks different up close, not quite what I was expecting. In the ring, she seemed so slender, much thinner than me. Now I can see that one of her thighs is almost as big as both of mine together. Muscular legs, strong upper body, except for her arms which seem soft, almost plump, not sculpted and trained. Feminine.

'Cheese,' she says to Nino, tipping her chin in the direction of the plates. 'You know it gives me indigestion.'

'Nathalie wanted to try it,' says Nino. 'You can have something else.'

'Oh, she's arrived, has she?'

'Her name's Nathalie,' Leon says.

Anna gives me a forced smile. She has lovely teeth. Perfectly straight at the front, small gaps on either side. Brilliantly white in this harsh lighting.

'How long are you staying?'

She has one of those husky voices I envy in other women.

'My contract says until the end of the year. But I don't have to stay until then,' I say, sensing that she'd rather not have me around for too long. I find her voice intimidating.

Anton comes back with a bowl of gherkins.

'It's up to you,' I add, not wanting them to doubt my commitment. 'I can leave just after the festival and meet my father for Christmas, or I can stay here with you.'

I pause for a moment.

'I don't really mind, either way. I like to go for walks, I'm fine wherever I am, I really don't mind. At least, I don't think I do.'

Another pause. I'm rambling.

'Watch out, Leon,' Nino says. 'Nathalie knows this town better than you do, she grew up here!'

'I only lived here for two years,' I say. 'From six to eight years old. I don't remember much about it. I came with my father, from Paris, just after my mother died. She had lung disease. He had a post teaching at the university in Vladivostok for two years.'

I keep talking, tell them his field is engineering physics, that he decided he'd rather work in a lab than teach. He had positions in San Francisco and Chicago after his stint in Vladivostok.

'He works with NASA now. He stayed in the US and I came back to Europe to go to school, I went to a boarding school in France, then I went to Belgium to study fashion design. I specialised in costumes for my final project.'

Leon asks if I've been back to Vladivostok at all since those two years. I shake my head.

'We never had a reason to come back. There was a woman called Olga who looked after me here while my father was at work but we lost touch with her. She's probably dead by now. She was very old. She was a French teacher, she'd retired.'

I'm waffling again. I'm trying to explain that I didn't actually choose to return. It's just the way things worked out. I was looking for work for the autumn and it just so happened that one of my supervisors knew the director of the circus in Vladivostok. He'd said there was a trio that needed someone for their costumes, so my supervisor recommended me.

'Leon got in touch with me, and here I am,' I say, throwing my hands in the air to indicate that it was pure chance.

'Still, it's wild that your supervisor knows the director,' Leon says.

'Apparently they worked together on a revival of *Cats* in London, a long time ago.'

'Leon's our guardian angel,' Nino says. 'He directs our routines, he understands how it all works. And he's responsible for operating Anna's safety equipment when we're training. He's in charge of the lunge. It's a really important skill.'

Leon looks down. Nino says there are currently fifteen trios doing Russian bar in the whole world. Five of them are seriously good, including themselves. He says it quite simply, without boasting. For the competition in Ulan-Ude, they're going to attempt the dangerous triple jump with Anna, four times in a row.

'Isn't that what you're doing already?'

'Not four consecutive jumps, one after the other,' Leon says. 'Without Anna getting down off the bar in between sets of two. The really hard thing is finding your balance again so quickly. And it's very demanding for the bases, it needs a great deal of strength.'

I glance at Anna. She's eating off Nino's plate.

'And if you win? What happens then?'

'Better money,' says Anton.

'We get noticed,' Nino adds. 'It's insurance for the circus directors, it means we have a better chance of being hired for big productions.'

'Leon says you've never worked in circus,' says Anna.

'He's right, I haven't.'

'It doesn't matter at all,' says Nino. 'We wanted a new team. It's a new routine, a whole new look.'

'Big festival,' Anton says. 'And first time for Anna too.'

Anna sinks back into her chair. I find it difficult not to stare at her thighs, the muscles so taut I want to throw a ping-pong ball at her leg and watch it bounce off. I turn towards the men and ask if they've already thought about the staging. Leon says they have a few ideas. They're thinking perhaps a leopard theme, Amur leopards. They're native to this region, more or less extinct. It's only an idea. They're open to any suggestions I might have. I promise to give it some thought. I offer to show them pictures of my work. The most recent ones, the work I'm most proud of, the costumes for Thomas's film for his diploma.

'He's a friend of mine on the film course,' I add.

I scroll through the pictures on my phone.

'Thomas wanted to make an underwater film,' I explain. 'But we didn't have enough money for the special effects. Filming underwater would have been much too expensive, so he decided to simulate it and leave everything visible, cables, rigging, it was all part of the concept. I did the same for my costume designs, I used aluminium foil and cellophane – we used so much cellophane, it stuck to everything, it was hopeless, we held it up either side of the camera, out of shot, so the actors could get into it, wrap themselves in it and wear it like water.'

I tell them the film's due to be shown at quite a few festivals. The four of them lean across the table, seemingly impressed. I scroll quickly through my stupid selfies, especially the ones where you can see Thomas kissing me on the neck. I blush, apologise for not having sorted through the pictures first.

'Will we be able to see it?' Leon asks.

'The film?'

'The film. Yes.'

'I don't think so,' I say, laughing. 'Not here in Vladivostok, what with all those top-secret submarines. I don't think it would go down too well.'

No one laughs. Anton gives me a disapproving look.

'But I do have it on my hard drive.'

We eat in silence. The canteen has emptied out. The young woman has pulled down the security grille in front of the counter. Muffled sounds drift towards us from inside the kitchen, surfaces being hosed down, the dishwasher droning.

'Do you go back to Kyiv sometimes?' I ask Anna.

'Of course.'

She slaps a fly away from her temple. She's cleaned Nino's plate. She stands up, says she's not feeling well, she's going back to her room.

'Will you be okay?' Nino asks.

She can't tell. It's probably just a passing thing. She looks over at me and says as she turns on her heels:

'At least, I hope that's all it is.'

THE NEXT MORNING, Anton is waiting for me at the artists' entrance. He surprises me by placing his hands on my shoulders and planting a kiss on my forehead, almost knocking me off my feet in the process. Nino and Anna are at the hospital, he tells me, we can go and wait in his room.

I stand in the doorway, hesitating. The room seems so small. He ushers me in with a wide sweeping gesture. Single bed, mustard-coloured walls, a small table and a chair piled up with clothes. A fridge hums in one corner. A suitcase lies open on the bed, Anton's personal belongings spilling out. The room is overheated – it's much hotter in here than elsewhere in the building. The atmosphere is stifling, the windows clouded with condensation. Anton clears the chair hurriedly and picks up a glass sitting at the foot of the bed.

'Wash,' he says in English as he heads out towards the men's bathrooms.

He comes back breathing hard, opens the fridge door wide and proudly shows me the contents. The fridge is stocked with fruit, cheese and bottles of water.

'Hungry?' he says.

I smile and say no thanks. He points at the drinks.

'Bubbles? No bubbles?'

I'll have some still water, I say, just to please him. He places an apple in my hand and closes my fingers around it. The apple feels refreshingly cool.

'Too hot in here,' he breathes as he perches on the edge of the bed.

He points at the ventilation grille on the ceiling. I can see it's not working. His chest rises and falls, the sound of his breathing fills the room. His hair is badly cut. He brushes it from his forehead, mops his face with his arm. The lines on his face seem to extend into the fabric of his shirtsleeve. His shirt is frayed in places from repeated contact with the bar. He has a lump on his right shoulder, highlighted by his posture. I can't help staring at it.

'Old injury,' he says.

My silence doesn't seem to bother him. I look down at the floor. Near the door is a small mound of wood shavings. Anton mimes the act of sculpting. He leans down under the bed and pulls out a suitcase full of shoe boxes, each one containing a miniature bird inside a carved wooden box. He tells me to pick one out. I gaze at them for a long time and select a bird that looks poised to take flight, its foot attached to the base by a fragile metal tab.

'Is this what you do in your free time?'

He nods vigorously.

'And of course, training.'

He bends down further, extracts a broom handle from under the bed and balances it upright in his open palm. He does the same with a pencil on his forehead, then on his nose. Eventually he puts them all down on the bed, turns to face the window and exclaims:

'Look!'

He moves his face closer to the windowpane. I do the same. The wind has dragged a wall of clouds over the ocean. A container ship sways lazily, a single point of colour in a grey tableau. There's a storm brewing. Anton glances at me, as if to confirm that I appreciate the grandeur of this scenery. I couldn't see much when I arrived yesterday, with daylight fading. To the right of the circus building, red-brick chimneys rise above a factory, 'Sugarsea' written in giant Latin letters. To the left, a great bridge looms in the mist.

'Biggest bridge,' Anton says. 'To Russky Island. You know?'

I nod. The island is just off the coast.

Leon walks in without knocking and finds us both standing with hands and forehead pressed to the window.

'What on earth are you doing?' he scoffs before letting us know that Anna and Nino are back.

We find them sitting in the risers. Nino has just had a heated exchange with the director, who is marching off looking furious. Anna limps after him, her calf muscles strapped with support tape. She walks straight past us without so much as a glance.

'Pulled muscle,' Nino says. 'Complete rest for a week. He'll pay us for the rest of the run so long as we appear in the parade at the beginning and end of every show.'

Leon rolls his eyes.

'What's the point of being in the parade if you're not performing?' I ask.

'Exactly,' Nino snaps.

'He's letting us rehearse here all autumn,' says Leon. 'So, we can't really object.'

'Tradition,' Anton adds and looks over at Nino.

'In the old days, when the circus came to town, you had to put yourself out there, make people want to come and see you,' Nino explains. 'It's pointless now, especially in a circus that's a permanent fixture. It doesn't really bother me, I'm from a circus family, my parents always said it was a mark of respect, a way of thanking the audience, but Anna finds it degrading to put herself on display like that. She's used to the world of elite sport, I think she'd rather we went ahead and performed the routine, even with the injury.'

'Could she do it?'

'Of course not.'

Anton shows me his damaged shoulder, says it all depends, he's never stopped even when he was injured.

'We can't all be like you,' Nino retorts.

Anton's injury happened the year of the Moscow Olympics, Nino tells me. Anton and his wife were rehearsing for the opening ceremony. They were doing a number on roller skates with a ribbon attached to the ceiling – his wife was an aerialist. One week before the big day she had a fall. She had a safety wire, but it hadn't been properly secured. Anton managed to catch her but he dislocated his shoulder. He ignored it and carried on so he could appear in the opening ceremony.

'That was in Soviet days,' Nino says. 'So, you know, things were different.'

'No, no,' Anton says. 'Duty. That's all.'

Nino carries on, irritated: 'By the time he saw a doctor, the muscles and tendons had healed themselves and it was too late to undo the damage.'

I stare at him in disbelief: 'Wasn't he in agony?'

'Of course, very painful!' Anton exclaims with a mixture of pride and resignation.

'Well,' Nino says, 'my father would make me go out and perform even if I had a fever of forty degrees. I was the director's son, I had to set a good example. If every performer stopped working at the slightest excuse . . . Actually it's not so bad, Anna being out of action. It'll give us more time to prepare for Ulan-Ude and we won't have to shorten our holiday. And we do need a rest.'

The saxophonist steps up onto the orchestra platform and unpacks his instrument. Anton says the orchestra are incompetent, he's glad he doesn't have to deal with them any more. Then the contortionist appears too, wearing a shiny tracksuit, an unruly child at her side. She starts warming up. Anton walks up to her, adjusts the position of her feet and shouts at the little boy to keep the noise down. The child clams up instantly. Nino leans over and whispers into my ear that Anton can't stop himself from trying to control everything, it's the coach in him. I keep my eyes on the woman in the centre of the ring. She rolls herself into a ball, head tucked against her stomach, limbs undulating like the tentacles of a sea anemone.

THE PERFORMERS line up backstage, heads held high. Leon parts the curtains. The parade moves forward into the ring. Leon watches on the video monitor. I stand beside him, eyes fixed on the screen. The wide-angle camera lens makes everything seem smaller. The seats are packed. The audience applauds, their hands seeming to flutter on the screen as the performers march in step, waving. One unit. Knees raised high, perfectly synchronised. On the second time round, they break rank and come back together to face the audience and walk backwards into the wings. It looks like a film being rewound.

THE STORM HASN'T BROKEN. I decide to go out and explore while I can. I wander through a park on a hill from which I can see the layout of the city, a network of hills sloping towards the shore with pink and alabaster streets threaded through them like ribbons on a wedding cake. As I move away from the centre of town, I pass more and more closed shutters. I go inside a church. A stall selling icons in the vestibule. I toy with the idea of buying one for my father but decide against it, I don't really know what they represent and taking him back a gift would mean letting him know where I've been. The nave is scattered with straw. No seats. Women come into the church, wrapped in shawls. They walk round once without stopping and go back out. I stand to one side and gaze at the stained glass. An official asks me to leave; he pats his hair: I'm not wearing a head-covering.

I walk back towards the hotel. Shopfronts devoid of window displays, nothing but posters to advertise their wares. On one, a picture of a dark-haired woman brandishing a razor, partly obscured by an image of a bunch of bananas outlined in black felt-tip. I push open the door cautiously, feeling like an intruder. Counters displaying cameras, jewellery, shoes. Sales assistants drinking tea, watching television. No one pays any attention to me. I walk over to the food section and examine the stacks of yoghurts on a shelf halfway down one aisle. Mont Blanc. I recognise the brand. Creamy vanilla. They should be refrigerated, shouldn't they? I check the wording on the package. Yes, I'm right. I place the yoghurt back on the shelf, picturing the harmful bacteria proliferating in the warmth of each pot, and buy bread and bananas instead. I go back to the hotel and eat them sitting on the floor in my room, using the bed in front of me as a table. It's not very comfortable, the bed is too high.

Through the walls I hear voices, a babble of unfamiliar tongues. Asian languages. Suitcases being moved around. Anton's bird box remains where I placed it on the bedside table. Close up like this, the small carved figure inside no longer looks like a bird. All I can see are marks made in the wood by the knife: the cuts representing wings, the body, the feet attached to the base. If I press my eye right up against the hole in the wall of the box, I can make out the two fine stalks on which sit the twigs that make up what must be the nest.

My mind turns to the task ahead of me: the costumes. I feel a rush of adrenaline. They've put their trust in me. It's an honour. I have very little experience. Ulan-Ude is coming up soon. All of a sudden, I'm assailed by doubt. We hardly know each other. The more I think about it, the more incongruous it seems. My role can't be that important if they feel they can hire someone completely unknown.

I watch the clips of their routine with Igor again. The camera is almost always on the flyer, hardly ever on the bases. Anton looks younger. He doesn't have that deep line across his forehead. But with the make-up and lighting it's hard to see much of his face.

BECAUSE OF the four daily parades the trio have to stay at the circus all day. I stick with Leon, watching him as he goes about his tasks. He is responsible for opening and closing the curtains, checking the condition of the lighting and safety equipment before each performance and keeping the snack trolleys filled. He complains about the students working on the tills; he says they act like they're on holiday. There's a plentiful supply of chocolate bars. Leon hands me one. I recognise the Sugarsea logo from the factory near the circus.

'Salted caramel,' he says. 'Sea salt with bits of seaweed. Completely inedible. The circus buys it because it's cheap.

It's all they buy these days. The plant's been there for fifty years. Prices slumped after anti-sugar campaigners claimed the building was reinforced with concrete that had children's cavity-ridden teeth mixed into it.'

'Seriously?'

He shrugs: 'Sugarsea was promoting its products as health-giving. Because of the seaweed in them.'

I tuck the chocolate bar into a pocket in my dungarees.

I go back and forth to my hotel several times a day. I don't eat with the group in the evenings, the canteen is too crowded. During the performances, Leon talks to me about himself. He's thirty-five. From Quebec. He started out teaching English at the circus school in Montreal. His students came from all over the world. He met a Russian tightrope-walker and they lived together while she finished her training. He learnt how to handle the safety equipment so he could operate her lunge and travel with her. When she decided she wanted to go back to Russia, he came too. They were hired by Vladivostok Circus and he ended up becoming an expert circus technician and performance director. When they broke up, he stayed on. He met Anna through her, in St Petersburg, where she was performing in a gala at the Hermitage Museum. It was thanks to him that Anna became a member of a trio with Anton and Nino. He's very proud of his role directing their act.

He keeps his voice down. I have to lean closer to hear what he's saying. I stare at his hands, the lines of veins on his forearms. He smiles apologetically. 'Not like you. I had to learn everything on the job.'

I snap back sharply that having a formal qualification doesn't necessarily make things any easier.

Three days to go until the last show. I've assigned myself the task of observing Anton and Nino as they train. I watch them from the stalls. They work on strength and flexibility. Nino rolls onto his back, raises his hips, toes pointed. Anton is less flexible. He doesn't have Nino's physique, his body is a solid mass of muscle that weighs him down and gets in his way when he is not carrying the bar. He rotates his hips slowly, hands on his waist. Anna stands between them. She throws a bag of sand up in the air for them to catch without making eye contact with each other. Then they work with the bar. She places a chair on the bar, balances it on two legs. They hold it in place for as long as they can, barely moving a muscle. Sometimes Leon is there with me. He explains to me why exercises of this kind are so important: the flyer has to rely entirely on the bases for balance and not try to stabilise herself at all. Think of Anna as the chair, he says, that's how passive she has to be. It's one of the hardest things about the Russian bar discipline:

'Anna had a hard time adapting because she was trained in trampoline. She was used to having a much larger surface to land on but with only her own skills to rely on. In Russian bar, you go much higher and you have only a few square centimetres to land on. I had the cold sweats when I first started lunging Anna. She'd shoot straight up to five metres above the bar. Thank God the harness was properly attached!'

I think back to what he told me about Igor. The accident. I don't dare ask them about it. I still don't know what happened.

The day of the final show. At the end of their training session, I walk over and have a good look at the bar. It's at least three metres long, wrapped from end to end in white tape with a strip of black tape marking the centre line where Anna has to be caught. I run my fingers over the bar. It feels rough. Tacky. Scuff marks from Anna's shoes. Nino walks over to me:

'Anton made it himself. Inside, there are three poles, like the ones pole-vaulters use.'

'Do all the groups make their own?'

'Yes, of course. They have to. There are so many things to take into consideration: the flyer's weight, height, level of skill.' He points to the sandbag flopped over the bar. 'You be Anna,' he says. 'Go on.'

I laugh in disbelief. Nino removes the sandbag, takes up his position, calls Anton. Then he looks at me and says:

'Up you get.'

Anton waves his hand at me, urging me on:

'Yes, try.'

'Another time,' I say, barely audibly.

'Okay,' says Nino, looking amused.

'Is it heavy?'

He places the bar on my shoulder. I feel its weight immediately, as if I'm struggling to lift a piece of furniture.

'Thirteen kilos, twenty-five with the carrying case. And with the impact from Anna, one hundred and fifty.'

'Is that all?' I thought it would be more than that.

Nino suddenly bears down on it. I stagger under the weight.

'Stop!' Anton shouts.

'I didn't hurt you, did I?' Nino asks, lifting the bar from my shoulder.

I rub my shoulder and shake my head, smarting from the pain.

The last parade is over. The doors open and the audience spills out into the street. We hear the clamour from inside the courtyard. Beyond the fence, the sun sinks into the ocean. There's a sudden rush of activity. The performers, their bags packed before the show, race off to catch trains, boats, buses to the airport. The staff all leave too – the cook, director, office workers and everyone else involved with the circus. Barely two hours later, we are alone. The light comes on outside, casting a glow on a fizzy-drink can jammed into one of the extraction vents. In the void created by all these departures the caravan seems to take up more space. I notice that it doesn't have any wheels. How could I not have spotted this before? The semi-circular recesses in the bodywork, bare axles beneath, biting into the earth like toothless jaws. Leon says the caravan was never intended to go on the road. The fencing was built around it. The whole structure would have to be dismantled to move the caravan out.

I start walking back to the hotel, feeling ill at ease. Before, with all the activity of the circus, my being away from the others seemed less conspicuous. I look back at the circus building silhouetted against the night sky. Stars glinting, reflected in the glass dome. The posters around the entrance have already been taken down. From the street, the flesh-coloured rotunda looks strangely human in form. It reminds me of a torso. A light comes on in one of the rooms. Anna's room. The men sleep on the courtyard side, overlooking the ocean. I picture Anna lit from behind, undressing, closing the curtains. The wind begins to swirl around me. I start to walk faster, pursued by a ray of moonlight.

PART II

TRAINING RESUMES. Nothing dangerous for this first session. Anna mounts the bar and bounces gently a few times. She takes a few tentative steps and then signals with a nod. The bases bend their knees and bear down on the bar. Anna spins her arms rapidly to find her balance as the bar flexes and retracts. From my ringside seat I can see the expression on her face, her eyes opening wider each time she rises, as if in surprise. Leon sits next to me, taking notes. Anton and Nino have their eyes fixed on Anna. I stare at Nino, his chest, solid shoulders, arms wrapped around the bar to extend his body towards Anton, their muscles contracting simultaneously. I can hear their breathing, especially the sharp exhalation that accompanies the effort on impact. They communicate in Russian, constantly interrupting each other. Anton gives directions, demonstrates a move to Nino, who listens, hands on hips, visibly impatient. Anna climbs back onto the bar. Their movements synchronise. Anna sets the beat, a rhythmic pulse, rising and falling, like breath being pushed out and sucked back into the lungs, a beating heart at the centre of the ring. She executes a few jumps, calls out to the others to stop. They adjust the bar and come together again. Anton speaks roughly to Anna, his tone insistent. She looks concerned, answers just as harshly. Leon translates for me: she's tired, she wants to stop for today, she thinks the bar is too flexible for what they want to do, she needs to gain sufficient height to have time to execute three turns, it's taking a toll on her legs, the demand made on them is enormous, she can still feel the effects of her injury. Anton insists she's overcompensating out of fear, she's afraid of being in pain, if she were to focus her attention on the goal she wouldn't hesitate.

They end their training session early.

I ask them to meet me in the canteen. I need to take their measurements, there's not enough light in the bedrooms. For the first time since I arrived, I'm the one taking the initiative. Anton appears, freshly showered, wearing flip-flops. He seems stockier, his body wider. Even his toes are thick, curved back on themselves. I measure him over his clothes, jot down the measurements in my notebook. Nino is next to make an appearance. He removes his T-shirt and trousers, strips down to his underwear. I wasn't expecting him to do this. Up close, he seems more fragile, despite the muscular physique. His right shoulder is purple, stained by years of training. The mark is reminiscent of a tyre print. Disconcerted, I lean in to wrap my arms around his chest. Caught off guard, he loses his balance, rights himself on one leg. I can see he's uncomfortable. We manage by each holding one end of the tape measure.

'Sorry,' he murmurs.

He waits behind me while I write down the numbers.

'You can get dressed again.'

He puts his clothes back on hurriedly, glances at Anna, who gives me a pointed look. She keeps her leotard on. Her skin is like porcelain, her arms marbled with veins. I don't dare touch her. I ask her to take her own measurements.

'That was impressive today,' I say, watching her as she adjusts the tape measure.

'Thank you.'

'Can you see the bar from all that way up there?'

'It happens very quickly, but yes, I can. I have to aim just right.'

'I could never do anything like that.'

She gives a short laugh.

'Thrust,' she says, handing me back the tape measure. 'I'm propelled by a combination of my own spring and the pressure the bases apply to the bar. The more they bear down, the higher I go. Without them, I wouldn't get much higher than a metre. I'd never get going.'

I open my laptop as soon as she leaves. Almost immediately I hear her calling me furiously from the corridor. I go out and look. There's no light. Everything is shrouded in darkness.

'You turned off the light!' she cries from the bottom of the stairs.

'I didn't touch anything,' I say as I turn the light back on.

'There's only one switch on each floor. If you turn it off, we have to walk all the way back to turn it on again!'

The light clicks off again. I point out to her that it's automatic. We couldn't tell before because of all the other performers constantly walking up and down.

Silence.

I hear a door slam.

IT'S AFTER eight o'clock when I leave the circus. Nino is leaning against the caravan, smoking. Fluorescent shoes, tailored jacket.

'You smoke?' I say in surprise.

'Too much. Aren't you staying to eat with us?'

I say I have work to do, wave goodbye and head for the centre of town. He follows me and falls into step beside me.

'You ought to take the bus at this time of night.'

'I need to walk.'

The road leads uphill. Darkened buildings, one or two with lights on in the windows. I unzip my jacket. The air temperature is still pleasant – cool but not cold. I can smell the sea.

'Was it okay, for you, this first session?'

He nods. They have a lot of work to do, but Anna is tough.

'The hardest part,' he says, 'is trust. With a flyer who's a beginner, you need two years to understand each other properly and be able to work without the harness. With a pro, it takes at least six months. It took five years for Anton and me to stop having to shout things out to each other all the time.'

I ask him if he knows why Anna cut short her career in sports to go and work in a circus. She pushed things too far, he says. Which is why she has a bad leg.

'The problem with sport is that you're always trying to break a record. We do it too but circus is less restrictive, there's more room for interpretation. It's not just technique being judged, there's the story too and the audience response. And costumes,' he adds with a wink. 'It all gets taken into consideration. And we don't have separate categories for men and women. Igor had everything. Speed, technique, talent. He was light too.'

He stops, as if regretting what he's just said.

He continues: 'Anton and I both thought we'd never find anyone to replace him. As soon as people hear the word "accident", that's it, however good your reputation is. And we were pretty well known too.'

I nod. Sensing my unspoken question, Nino carries on talking:

'It was during a training session. We'd been working for months. We were ready. There was a moment when we could tell Igor was tired. We were all tired. We should have stopped for a break. It's the responsibility of each individual to know just how far they can go. You can't let yourself be surprised by something like a cramp. Igor knew that. He'd always worked without safety equipment, from really early on. He never wanted to rely on the lunge for security. When the flyer wants to stop jumping, they bend their knees to absorb the recoil of the bar and the bases stop applying pressure to the bar. You have to shout stop. That's the signal. Igor shouted. But he shouted a thousandth of a second too late. I don't know what happened. He veered off to one side. When you're being pushed up into a jump, Anton and I have to already know where you're going to land so we have time to be ready to catch you directly underneath. If you get the jump wrong, even if you land on your head, you need to be caught by the bar. It won't save you, but it will at least absorb your fall. Igor was catapulted ten metres off to the side. He crashed directly onto the ground.'

'He survived . . .' I begin.

'He went back to college. He's working in a village on Lake Baikal, in the museum in the nature reserve.'

'He had to give up circus?'

'He had his spine fused. He can't raise his head.'

'Do you know how he is?'

'Anton sees him occasionally. He says he's doing okay.'

I nod.

'I don't know though,' Nino adds. 'We haven't seen each other since it happened.'

He stumbles and grips my arm. I look down and recognise the cat from the circus, the skinny one, with pink skin. The cat rubs up against my legs. Nino picks it up.

'Leon should keep it indoors,' he says.

'Is it his?'

'Yes. Don't tell me you petted the thing, it'll never stop following you around.'

We start walking again.

'Aren't you ever scared?' I ask after a while.

'All the time,' he says. 'I'm terrified with every new jump. Scared of getting hurt. Scared of hurting Anna. I'm scared of the audience too; I get stage fright. I think it's a good thing though. You become more aware of what's going on. You don't make so many mistakes.'

He shifts his hold of the cat.

'I'm banking on it all working out in Ulan-Ude. Money-wise, we can't go on touring like this year after year.'

'And if things don't go according to plan? What will you do then?'

'Carry on as we are. Try and get as much circus work as we can and keep on training for the following year. If that doesn't work, I don't know. My parents would love it if I took over the family circus.'

'Is that what you want?'

He takes a deep breath.

'It's been in the family for three generations,' he says, explaining that the whole operation will grind to a halt if he doesn't take it on. He's an only child.

'But running a circus is more complicated than it used to be,' he says. 'Audiences are good sometimes, especially during school holidays, but the cost of renting the space just goes up and up. Berlin and Cologne are impossible, Geneva and Zurich completely out of the question. Caravans have to be squeezed right up against each other. To economise on space.'

He laughs and says his father's become an expert at that.

'Three years ago, the circus went bankrupt. They managed to carry on with the help of donations and now they survive by renting out the big top for private events. Weddings, corporate receptions, that kind of thing.'

He stops. I don't know what to say.

'I don't want my father to end up doing his act at a car show and having to stop halfway through because no one gives a damn,' he says forcefully. 'When I was a kid people couldn't wait for us to come to town, and not just at Christmas. Now, people see us as street performers, fairground entertainers.'

I don't say anything. He's right in a way. I can't deny that I've always seen circus as inferior to theatre or dance. I don't really know why.

'Whenever I get fed up with Anton, I start missing my family. I miss my mother's home-made chips, I miss having a drink after shows. I even miss the lack of privacy. But then I remember how glad I am to get away from them. Working with the trio is completely different. It's a whole other level. Whenever I go home to the family circus for the holidays, you can bet that after two days I'll develop tendonitis or pains in the hips! And I'm not yet thirty years old. Crazy, I know! Seriously, sharing a caravan with God knows who, it's all very well for a while. But I want to be able to bring a guy back without having to ask for permission.'

I'm not sure how to respond. After a few moments I confess that seeing all of them every day is already more intimacy than I'm used to. I've always lived alone, apart from when I lived with my father when I was little. Even when I was away at school, I had my own room.

'And you don't mind leaving your fiancé?' he says. 'And taking off halfway across the world?'

'Thomas is not my fiancé.'

'I knew an Italian who always referred to his boyfriend as his fiancé, even when they'd only been out once. But I get it,' he adds, seeing my embarrassment, 'you've run away, all the way to Vladivostok.'

'I broke up with him before I left.'

We're walking through an area where the pavement is being dug up. I step carefully, avoiding the holes:

'You know, when you're a student, you end up getting together with people without really intending to. I mean obviously, you have things in common, but . . .'

'It's sort of the same everywhere,' Nino says.

'Probably. Anyway, my coming here had nothing to do with him.'

I think for a moment:

'It's funny. I've never had to worry about finding work. I'm starting a new job in January, I've been hired by the Théâtre National de Bretagne, I'm going to be an assistant to the artistic director. I could have taken some time off. Maybe I should have done. I like the stage though. I mean, I like seeing people wearing my creations. But I don't know. I feel tired somehow. Maybe it's because I've spent five years studying, having to analyse everything. I needed to change direction, work with performance in a completely different way.'

'Without having to think,' Nino says.

'That's not what I meant.'

'What's wrong with that?' he says, unperturbed. 'The body has an intelligence of its own.'

We've reached the hotel. A couple are having their picture taken in the old-fashioned wedding carriage near the restaurant entrance. The woman has her foot stuck, her stocking is caught in the step. She's wearing fishnet tights. Their criss-cross pattern makes me think of meat roasting on a spit.

'So this is where you've been coming to escape from us,' Nino says, teasing me.

I react defensively, tell him I'm glad I came to Vladivostok:

'I'm enjoying working with all of you. I like the idea that I'm adding a bit of poetry to what you do, helping you satisfy the audience's need for fantasy and . . .'

'You think so?' Nino says, cutting me off mid-sentence. 'I think people come to see if it's all going to work,' he adds. 'They want to see how far we can go. It's easy to say they're hoping for something magical but the truth is, what they really want is for something to go wrong. People find it reassuring to see others make mistakes.'

His face is hidden in the shadows. The cat is asleep in his arms. It looks like it might be dead. I thank Nino for walking me home and tell him he doesn't need to do it every day.

'Come and stay at the circus,' he says. 'The bedrooms are rubbish but the caravan isn't bad at all. We've been using it to store things but we could easily fix it up to make you comfortable. You'd have your own space.'

I try and picture the setting, embarrassed at feeling exposed. He's probably right. It's absurd for me to stay at the hotel now. But then Anna's image flashes through my mind. I'll think about it, I say.

I ARRIVE the next morning to find Nino bringing a chair out of the caravan. Leon is wringing out a dish-cloth over a bowl of dirty water, he's been cleaning the windows. He tells me they haven't been able to hook up the electricity. There's no water either.

'You'll have to share the girls' changing area with Anna,' Nino adds cheerfully, 'and we can all eat together in the canteen. You'll still be better off than at the hotel. Take your time getting set up, we can do without you for our training session. You can go and get your things from the hotel.'

Anna comes out of the circus building with a cup of coffee in her hand.

'They haven't slept all night,' she says cryptically.

The caravan is perfect for me, a house in miniature. Dark brown curtains, walls painted yellow with flying-duck motifs. A space that's tiny, but functional. I fold down the shelf, place my sewing machine on it, my shoes on the floor just beneath. I hang my dungarees and coat over the back of the toilet door, fold the rest of my clothes and stow them in the sink along with my underclothes. My tools go on top of the stove. I sit down on the narrow little bed. Not big enough for two people. I dismiss the thought. The mattress is hard, unyielding, the blanket held down with elastic at the corners, like a stretcher. I stand up and open the curtains, gaze at the jumble of items piled up in the courtyard, the assortment of clutter they'd been housing in the caravan. It was kind of the boys to let me have this space. I'm touched. I realise I've forgotten to thank them.

The cloakrooms on the first floor of the circus building remind me of the changing areas in old outdoor swimming pools. Bare brick walls, metal lockers, a sink unit with two basins, a large mirror above it. The showers are behind a partition, separated by ancient curtains that are discoloured from being dragged across the wet tiles.

Mould starting to bloom on the grouting. I dab it lightly with my finger and it vanishes.

When I arrive at the ring, they've already finished their training session. They've all left except for Leon, who is busy with a lunge and a harness, checking that everything is as it should be. They'll be using the equipment tomorrow, he says. Today's session went better than the previous day's. Perfecting a routine takes time. I look up at the stage above the artists' entrance. Empty except for the double bass. It belongs to the circus, Leon explains. The director decided it was more cost-effective to buy an instrument that could be used and reused than to hire a professional bass player.

I start to explain my thoughts for the costumes. The inspiration for Anna's comes from Cats. Nothing too original. I've been thinking mostly of the practical aspects. Lycra, with an outer layer of fine velour. A tail attached to the belt, a headband for the ears, hair drawn back tight. Not a leopard, that would be too trite. She should be all in black. A panther. We'd have to pay special attention to her make-up. I'll practise. For the bases, I'm still trying to work something out. I'm thinking something solid, to symbolise Siberia and its forests. Conifers, birch trees. A military jacket, a woven fabric in a dark colour. People aren't looking at their bodies. I'll concentrate on their heads. Their heads as an extension of the bar. Branches. A system of branches attached to a helmet. Leon likes my idea. He hasn't choreographed the act yet, but he'll follow my lead. I feel encouraged, get carried away, talk about how I see Anna as majestic, the big cat leaping through the air. I'll need only basic materials. I've seen a military surplus shop that shouldn't be too expensive. He says he'll come with me.

'Now?' I say.

'I think it's closed.'

He checks on his phone, it's closed, we can go there early next week.

'What are you doing now?' he asks.

Caught off guard, I offer to cook. Great idea, he says, it was meant to be his turn. He's going for a walk, he says. I'm not invited to join him.

I spend the afternoon walking all over town, wandering from one grocery shop to another, unable to make up my mind. In Brussels, I lived on sandwiches and basic salads.

Thomas and I had a semblance of a life as a couple, we sometimes cooked together, but he preferred to be left alone to get on with it. He's an excellent cook, he'd use ingredients I'd never even heard of and he was thrilled when he found things like sweet woodruff or sumac. He explained to me what all the different leaves, berries, roots and pods were. I should have listened to him. I buy some rice and onions to make a risotto. Ignoring the cost, I add a large fillet of smoked salmon. I tell myself I'll be more frugal next time.

THAT EVENING, Leon suggests we celebrate my moving in by watching my film on a big screen; we can use the projector he found while he was clearing out the caravan. Nino helps him rig up a sheet in the canteen while Anna and I arrange the chairs in a semicircle. The cat struts in front of the projector, casting a huge shadow over the screen. Anton is irritated. Leon pulls the cat onto his lap. We watch as the actor presses a button inside his pilot's cabin and blows a submarine to smithereens. Loud sounds of explosions. The camera lingers on his face. The film is a series of single-shot scenes. I don't remember them being so long. Divers inside a warehouse, wrapped from head to foot in cellophane that expands and contracts as they breathe. They move with slow, ponderous steps, simulating weightlessness. They look like jellyfish weighted down with lead.

'Thomas wanted to do something satirical, a war film but in a sci-fi style.'

Leon says he thinks that's rather ambitious.

'It's been quite well received,' I say, defensively. 'In festivals, I mean. It's all relative. You have to have a certain level of background knowledge to really appreciate this kind of film.'

'Such as?' Anna asks.

'No, I mean there's no reason why you wouldn't understand the film,' I say, backtracking hurriedly. 'I wasn't talking about you.'

I try and explain that it's a different sphere, like circus is for me:

'It's not my thing, I'm not used to it I mean. The first time I ever went to a circus I knew it wasn't for me, when I was about eight or nine. It was a school trip.'

I tell them that I see it all very differently now, since I've been working with them.

'And it wasn't even a proper circus I saw back then. It was more of a freak show, the kind you see in old films, when they still made a spectacle of people with deformities, or put animals on display, like hippos for example.'

I stop myself suddenly. I've been talking too much again, out of embarrassment.

'Yes, that kind of thing was all the rage a hundred years ago,' Anna says. 'In America.'

The credits roll over stills from the film. A shot of me on a red carpet with Thomas, his arm round my waist. They clap when my name comes up. I cover my face with my hands.

'Why don't you film us?' Nino asks. 'We usually work with a fixed camera but maybe you could track our movements, do some close-ups.'

I tell him I don't know, I don't have any equipment, I'm not a film director.

'We know that,' Anna says.

'All you need is a phone,' Leon adds. 'You don't have to create beautiful images, just something to help us correct any weaknesses. I can't do it – I'm going to have to lunge Anna.'

I end up agreeing to do it.

'Your dad must be proud of you,' Nino says from over by the window, where he's having a smoke.

'I wouldn't know about that. The day of the screening

he was busy working out how to get a plane to fly without any fuel.'

'How did that go?'

'It crashed after the first hundred metres.'

'What exactly is it that he does?' Leon asks.

His interest in my father takes me by surprise. I haven't thought about what he does in years. It's not something I talk to people about. He's an engineering physicist, his field is ionic propulsion. I launch into an explanation. Polarisation, electric current, energy. I try and give an accurate description but I want to convey the beauty of what he does too. I talk about how my father is fascinated by the microscopically small, about his work with NASA on the infinitely large, about how he tried to get me to understand the principle of polarisation using Smarties when I was little by throwing them in the air for me to catch them in my mouth, and then explaining that sugar attracts human mouths in the same ways as ions attract or repel one another and create a current.

'He's at MIT, working with NASA. They're trying to get solid bodies to fly without using any fuel. So long as they aren't too heavy, that is.'

I'm starting to repeat myself. I don't know if I'm making any sense. I tell them he's interested in satellites in orbit. I talk about space, ecological concerns, thrust, gravity. I know I'm oversimplifying.

'Basically,' I say, pausing to catch my breath, 'my father is experimenting with the properties of air and trying to find a way to get things to fly without using any kind of fuel.'

'In Russia, they've made a train move by the power of thought,' Anton declares in perfect English.

The others don't respond. I continue, cautiously:

'Anyway, on a microscopic scale, there's been a revolution in understanding, but there's still huge progress to be made. We're a long way from powering aircraft.'

'How can people work on something when they know they'll never see it actually come to fruition?' Anna asks.

'I know,' I say. 'I couldn't work like that.'

I look past the black screen out into the night sky visible through the glass dome.

'And to think that up there, we can see things that stopped existing a long time ago, like the light from dead stars.'

I carry on, saying whatever comes into my head:

'When we were in Chicago, the wind kept blowing my father's hat off and he'd run after it. Once he was almost knocked over by a bus, so I sewed weights into the brim.

He was so happy he bought me a sewing machine, a portable one, I brought it with me, and now it's here, in the caravan. By the way, thank you. I haven't thanked you yet. For the caravan.'

I stop myself again, flustered.

'Shall we eat?' Anna says.

The risotto has cooled down and dried out. Leon says we could reheat it by adding hot water. Nino says no, you can't reheat risotto. Anton arranges the food on our plates, using a cup to shape the rice into mounds, like crème caramel. I've made far too much. I weighed out two hundred grams of rice per person. Anton says he thinks it's fine, it'll keep him and Nino anchored to the ground. Anna shouldn't eat too much of it though, she won't be able to jump. She mimes punching him in the shoulder. I'm worried that it's not salty enough. Anna thinks it's just right. People in Europe salt their food too much, she says.

'Delicious,' says Leon.

I watch them helping themselves to more, thinking about what Anna has just said, the way she sees Russia as separate from Europe. I realise I think of this country sometimes as European and sometimes as Asian. I'm not sure where I'd put it now. Everything would be so much simpler if continents were defined only by the oceans that border them.

The conversation turns to films. We don't have many common reference points. Before long I stop trying to join in and just listen. Leon switches off the neon lights and we carry on in the glow of a couple of lanterns. Nino does his best to translate the jokes for me. By the end of the evening, I'm exhausted but relieved to see the substantial dent they've made in my dish.

Dear Papa,

Our apartment is on Rue de la Muse. It has four rooms, plus the cellar and attic. It's spacious. And very bright. Your grandson has his own room. We've been here for two days. You'd be shocked at the mess we're in, I've never been good at moving, nothing is in boxes, I've stuffed everything into shopping bags and suitcases. For the moment, the bags are all sitting in the part of the flat where their contents will eventually be used. We're up on the fourth floor. We can't hear the noise from the street. Thomas has already brought some of the furniture up, but not enough to muffle the sound of our footsteps.

WE SETTLE into a routine. Practice sessions take place just before lunch or in the early part of the afternoon. They consist mainly of a series of jumps with slight variations. I have a hard time distinguishing between them. Before they shoulder the bar, Anton and Nino talk to each other in Russian for what seems like ages. I'm bored after two sessions. They've said several times that I don't need to be there, so I put in a short appearance and then leave. I've set up my workstation in the canteen.

We've organised a rota for the chores. We take it in turns hoovering the common areas: hallways, canteen, cloakrooms. We do the same for meals but Nino always makes too much and messes up the rota. It happened the first time with me too. Anton uses the leftovers to make delicious soups. I just wish he wouldn't smother everything in cream. Anna sprays whipped cream on everything; she eats it straight from the aerosol can, which she never cleans. She doesn't cook, her job is to load the dishwasher. She waits until it's completely full. There are enough place settings for the whole canteen so the dishes pile up all week. The smell gets really overpowering. Then she turns on the moving belt and all our dirty dishes start to glide slowly past, as if there were a hundred of us. It amuses her to watch them vanish behind the rubber curtain that protects against splashing, but I find it slightly alarming, I don't quite understand why. I resist the urge to do the washing-up myself, I don't want her to get the impression I'm belittling her.

We spend evenings in the canteen, where it's warm and the internet connection is strongest. Anton works on his little wooden boxes. The bird is joined by a series of animals. He doesn't worry about them being realistic, the weasel is bigger than the deer, and the she-wolf looks less threatening than either of them. Nino and Anna sit and watch Russian films on a laptop. They bring blankets from their bedrooms and make themselves a cosy nest. When I asked Nino what one of the films was about, he spent hours trying to find subtitles in English. Ever since then, I've tried not to show any interest. I download radio programmes about Russian history and listen to them but the narrators put me to sleep with their gloomy delivery. I stop myself from looking up Thomas's profile on social media. Leon reads a lot. When I ask him to lend me some books, he gives me everything by Jack London. Sometimes the four of them stay up late, talking. They start out in English and slide into Russian. Leon worries that I don't say much. I tell him not to worry. I like listening to them, even when I can't understand. When I do join in, they stop and listen, patiently at first, but by the time I've finished saying what I have to say, they've usually moved on to another topic. By the end of the evening, they all have their headphones on. They each go back to their own room listening to music. I put my headphones on too, but without any music. I sit there, focusing on the sounds inside my own head. It makes me feel closer to the others somehow.

THE MILITARY SURPLUS store is on the main street. Leon and I wander among the displays: naval jumpers, military caps, mosquito-repellent sprays, magnets. Weapons and related items are in a separate room. I browse through the clothing, hold articles up against myself. Everything is made of heavy fabrics and sliding the hangers along the rack is hard work. I find some canvas and burlap fabric, helmets and black trousers for Anton and Nino. I try on a belt for Anna. I'm a bit thinner than she is but my waist is less well-defined than hers. It'll be perfect for her. Leon places a packet of dog food down next to the till. I give him a questioning look. He says Buck will eat anything.

On our way out of the shop I mention that I need some twigs and branches for Anton and Nino's headgear. Leon suggests we go out to Russky Island. We take a bus across the bridge, get off near the shore at the edge of the forest. It's colder here. The shore is lined with fortress walls concealed in the rock face, artillery guns pointing towards Japan. The city looks even more fragmented from here, the bridge seems immense. We can make out the circus, the Sugarsea factory. Leon points to the far side of the island:

'That's the new university campus. They moved it over there. The bridge hasn't been here that long, you had to get here by ferry before. Everything began to change a few years back when the city hosted a summit on trade in the Far East. The whole place has been transformed. It's much easier now for students to commute from Vladivostok. But there still aren't that many Russians at the university. Most of the students still come from China, Japan and Korea and live on campus. The bridge didn't make any difference to that.'

'So where do the Russians go to university?'

'Mostly to Moscow, I think, or St Petersburg. At least, that's what people around here say.'

While we're collecting branches Leon asks me about myself. I tell him about all the times I've moved, about life at boarding school in France. I say how much I liked it all, despite the difficulty I had in making lasting friend-ships. He listens, brows furrowed, trying hard to make out what I'm saying against the wind. I pause and think for a moment when he asks me what made me want to work in costumes and not fashion.

'That's a good question,' I say. 'It's probably because I don't particularly like telling stories, I can help shape a narrative but I can't create one from scratch. I'm not so interested in what an outfit says. I prefer working with the actual human form. I suppose it's all to do with design. I'd feel too restricted by fashion. I did a course once in a home for the elderly where I had to learn how to clothe all kinds of bodies: amputees, people with dwarfism, people who were flabby, muscular. I found it gratifying when people were happy with what I did. It made me wonder what it would be like to work in a hospital. With serious burns victims, for example. I might even be able to make a vital contribution.'

I must sound so pretentious, I think to myself. But Leon seems interested.

The water laps at the shore, black foam building up around our feet. I start talking again, without prompting this time, about the two years I spent here, with Olga: the smell of frying that filled her apartment day and night, how she started cooking first thing in the morning, boiled eggs, cheese pancakes puffed up with cooking oil that she poured away down the shower afterwards. She was always cleaning but the shower was still grimy, her eyesight wasn't that good, she was old. She gave me buttermilk all the time, I told her I drank it but in fact I gave it to the dog, a wiry little creature that looked more like a goat. I loathed buttermilk, the word itself made me feel ill, the colour and that slightly acidic taste. She had a photo of her son over the television, holding his diploma, the seal prominently displayed, you could tell it was a photocopy, the paper was dark around the edges, the way it looks if the scanner isn't closed properly and light gets in. I never actually saw the son.

We draw level with a man fishing. In the windscreen of his van are two knitted dolls, a couple, the palms of their hands stitched together, orange hair, the woman's breasts disproportionately large, the man bald, with a moustache.

Leon climbs up a rock towards a blackened, leafless bush. Its branches are brittle. He chooses carefully and comes back down with his arms full. He eyes up my meagre haul. I've been too busy watching him. We crouch down, foreheads touching, and sort through the branches. We snap pieces off, keep the sturdiest ones and throw the rest into the undergrowth.

'What about your boyfriend? Doesn't he mind you being so far away?'

'Thomas? He's not my boyfriend.'

Leon raises his eyebrows.

'It's fine,' I say. 'He's starting to get a bit of recognition internationally. He's found someone to produce his next project, a full-length fictional feature, I'm happy for him.'

'It must be good for you too?' Leon says.

'It doesn't affect me at all.'

'Don't you want to work with him any more?'

I laugh bitterly.

'No one works *with* Thomas. They work *for* him.'

I picture all those actresses. He has plenty of people around him, I say. He doesn't need me. Leon stares at me, eyes wide. I try and think of a response, but he's already looking away. He says he wishes he'd had that kind of foresight at my age. I ask him what he means. He tells me he broke up with his girlfriend the year before. I hadn't realised it was so recent.

'She said she wasn't interested in having children. Three months later she was pregnant by someone else, another tightrope walker, they'd been working together on a routine. They were getting married. She wrote and told me,' he says. 'She was still performing when she was five months pregnant.'

'Did you ever see her again?'

'We ran into each other in the spring. At a festival. She'd just had her baby, she was already back at work.'

'And?'

He shrugs:

'Sometimes these things get better with time. But I can't help feeling that it's getting harder for us to even say hello to each other. We treat each other like strangers, it's as if we've never even met. That's the way it goes, I guess. It's not the end of the world, is it?'

He pauses. Since all this happened, he says, he's gone off the whole circus scene, it's all lies, a forest of lies.

'Like these branches, you mean?'

Leon gives a little smile.

'You're putting words in my mouth. What I mean is, all these people who rely on secrets to protect their tricks, sometimes it just goes too far for me. Nino's had an inner ear problem. He's told Anton and me about it, but not Anna. It was important for her not to know.'

'Why was that?'

'It could have spooked her. Can you imagine? If she started having doubts about either of her bases?'

I ponder this in silence, uncertain as to whether I'm expected to comment. We start walking back towards the bridge, the wind harsh against our faces. My jumper rides up as I walk. I feel the evening chill on my midriff.

'They know what they're doing,' Leon adds definitively.

WE RETURN to the smell of grilled chicken wafting through the halls. I go up to the canteen, taking my laptop with me. Anton is stirring a reddish-coloured soup, thickened with big chunks of carrots and onions. I'm hungry. He ladles some into a bowl for me and adds cream and a sprig of dill. He opens the oven and takes out a chicken. Someone's already made a start on it, there's a leg missing. Anna ate it, he says. He slices off the other leg and serves it to me on a bed of rice. As he puts the cream away in the fridge, I notice that the shelves are stacked with discounted yoghurts. Anton sits down at the other end of the table, arms folded across his chest.

'What about you?' I ask him in English.

'Later. With Nino.'

He closes his eyes, turns to the table which is too low to fit his legs under and instead stretches them out towards the windows. The wind is picking up. A cloud of dust spirals upwards towards the dome. A shutter slams. The chicken is enormous, the leg takes up half my plate. Bones surrounded by tendons, pockets of rice, muscle. An assortment of flesh-toned hues, complementary colours harmoniously arranged. I'm seized by an urge to burst out laughing. Chicken thighs. Anna's thighs.

Anton hasn't moved since I sat down to eat. He looks sleepy. I rinse off my plate, knife and fork, check to see if he's actually asleep. I turn my attention to the yoghurts, arranging them in order of colours – plain, vanilla, caramel, coffee, chocolate – before opening up my email inbox. I'm waiting to hear from the Théâtre National de Bretagne. I'd like to have some time to get ready for the job before I start in January. I haven't looked at my emails since I arrived in Vladivostok; my throat tightens at the sight of all the unopened messages. I'll come back to them later. I check my social media. Thomas has posted a picture of himself with a girl – an English actress, my age, lipstick, black hair. I linger on the picture. They seem so far away. I think about Leon's ex. I type 'tightrope walker' into the search engine and bring up pictures of high-wire acts, illustrations for children's books, puffy clouds tinged with blue. Dream-like. Clichéd. I find them strangely disconcerting.

Nino arrives and I shut down all the open windows. His jacket makes a whooshing sound as he peels it off and says:

'God, it's windy out there!'

He looks over at Anton sleeping and sighs.

'He was waiting for you,' I say.

'I know. It's the same every time. He sends me out on an errand and then forgets all about it. It's ridiculous. I don't really mind though. I'm quite happy to do stuff for him. It's better for everyone if I just do what he wants.'

'Where were you?'

'At the bank. Anton's always forgetting his PIN. He changes it just about every week. We're already into November and he needs to send money to Igor urgently.'

'To Igor?'

'Yes.'

'Why?'

Nino stares at me, as if he's trying to work something out.

'Nathalie,' he says eventually. 'Igor's his son.'

'What?'

He smiles ruefully. He thought I knew. The audience never realised it either. With his solid build, Nino's the one who looks more like Anton. Igor's frame was birdlike.

'There was quite a bit of tension between him and Anton, I'm not really sure what it was all about. Igor really liked it in the US. Out of all the countries we travelled to, America was his favourite. We worked for Cirque du Soleil in New York for a whole year once.'

He pauses.

'It wasn't like this, that's for sure,' he says, gesturing to indicate our surroundings. 'Anton started turning down contracts from the US soon afterwards. We never really knew why. Igor and I were twenty-two. I think Anton was afraid Igor would leave us and take a permanent contract with Cirque du Soleil, in Las Vegas. He was starting to get offers from them. I don't really know though. Anton was always pushing him. We were working on doing the triple jump six times.'

He pauses again.

'There were some very nasty articles in the Russian papers after the accident. Journalists claiming that Anton would rather see his son disabled than leaving for the US.

You know,' he says as I stare at him in disbelief, 'Anton was a big star in Russia. He and his wife used to perform at all the great state occasions.'

Anton starts to breathe more deeply in his sleep.

'How does he carry on?' I ask, thinking out loud. 'How can he go on performing after his son's accident?'

Nino gets to work picking the rest of the meat off the chicken. Eventually, Anton wakes with a start. Nino serves two generous plates. Anton holds his up to show me and points at the carcass. I smile:

'I already ate,' I say.

'You did? Oh, right!'

I'M NOT SURE what to do with myself in my free time. I can't remember ever having so much of it. Over the past few years, I've had one commitment after another. I was always thinking ahead to the next project. And when I first arrived here I spent most of my time getting to and from the hotel. I play with the cat, musing about my surroundings. I can't work until I've made sure everything is clean and tidy. I start with a quick blitz of the caravan and move on to the common areas. The bathrooms are riddled with mould. Whenever I take a shower, I feel like all I'm doing is feeding the mushrooms.

Anna and I stand in front of the mirror to brush our teeth. The fan comes on when you turn on the light. The noise it makes drowns out the sounds of our gurgling and spitting. Anna has lined up all her creams and potions on her side. There's a clear dividing line. On my side, there's nothing but a tube of toothpaste and some adhesive for the false eyelashes I was planning to give her.

I watch Anna as she rinses and spits. Then, she plunges her fingers into a large tub of body lotion and spreads it over her face. She's changed for the night. A thigh-length man's T-shirt with a date and something written in Russian on it: 'goth police'. I bring my face closer to the mirror. The psoriasis hasn't spread any further, but the blistering is worse. Anna points at her lotion, says I can use it. I open my mouth to say thank you and toothpaste comes dribbling out. I'd forgotten I hadn't finished brushing.

'Wait for me?' she says.

She scuttles towards the toilets further down the corridor. I press the light switch periodically to make sure it stays on. As I undress, I take the opportunity to examine myself. Crinkled skin on the back of my thighs, faint lines across my lower abdomen, stretch marks. Skinny and flabby at the same time, I say to myself. I feel cold. I hop up and down on the tiled floor, pull on my pyjamas, the green ones I've had since I was thirteen.

Anna comes back, walking like a dancer, on her toes, shoulders hunched.

I'M WOKEN one night by the sound of the cat mewling, its cry distorted by the wind. I open the door to let him in. He jumps up on the bed, licks himself, peeling off what little fur he has left. I get back into bed and he curls up on the pillow. His breath smells foul. I can't sleep for his purring. I pick him up carefully by the scruff of the neck like a mother cat, supporting him under the belly with the other hand and place him back out on the doorstep. The wind is gusting in the courtyard, the chairs have been overturned. I stand there with the cat until I start to feel too cold. He can get back inside the circus through a flap in the ventilation system that Leon keeps open with a rock. I go back inside and close the door. I can hear him wailing underneath the caravan. The sound is soon drowned out by the wind. I feel guilty. I imagine him bristling with energy, a tiny, futile engine for this caravan without wheels.

MID–NOVEMBER, my mock-ups for the costumes are ready. I arrive early at rehearsal, draping the costumes over a row of seats but the weight of the antlers makes them look lopsided, so I spread them out on the ground instead. I'm just finishing as the others arrive. After a few exclamations of surprise, they begin to inspect the details. Anton and Nino try on their jackets. Anna goes off to one side to put on her bodysuit.

'It's fine,' Nino says. 'A little stiff perhaps.' He raises and lowers his shoulders.

I make some adjustments to the collar, the length at the hips, tell him it will loosen up.

'How long will that take?' he asks.

Anton says his sleeves are stiff too. I take note of their comments. I'll have to make some changes. They should try and imagine the costumes together with the make-up, I tell them. I was thinking of something green and white to represent the birch trees you see everywhere in Russia.

Anna appears. The clingy black suit accentuates her shape. The velour makes her shapely thighs and flattened chest shimmer. The sleeves narrow to a point, held in place by a piece of elastic around the forefinger. Anna does a twirl, the panther's tail, light and springy, spinning in her wake.

'It's a bit tight, don't you think?' she says.

I check the tension at the elbows, shoulders, the zipper down the back.

'It all seems fine to me.'

I glance at Leon for approval. He says nothing, chin in hand. Anna asks Nino what he thinks of the velour. I start having doubts. In certain lights, this kind of fabric can take on an aspect of animal hide or wet fur. Anton and Nino have donned their headgear. The antlers are longer than I'd imagined them. They look like antennae. Nino thinks they're gorgeous but he's afraid they could be unsafe; they're heavy, they pull on the back of the neck when he looks up.

'Not bad,' Anton says, shaking his head and making his antlers wobble.

Seeing him encased in that jacket, I can't help thinking he looks like a cockroach. I gather everything up hastily, muttering that they're only test models. Anna says she doesn't want the tail, she could trip on it. Leon finally breaks his silence. He's not sure about the idea of the panther. He needs to think about it some more. Anna turns to face me. She doesn't want the belt either, she doesn't want anything constricting her abdomen. She has to be able to move freely in her costume, she shouldn't be aware of it at all. It should be like a second skin. She places her hands on her waist and sucks in her stomach:

'Do you understand what I'm talking about?' she says. 'Do you think you can do it?'

IN THE CANTEEN, I fling the costumes down on the table. I start undoing them, taking them apart. How was I supposed to know? This circus business is all new to me. Leon didn't give me any help at all. He knew what I was planning to do with these costumes, I'd talked to him about my ideas. I put away my tools, pins, needles, thread, laughing bitterly to myself. How could I have been so stupid? Those antlers are far too heavy. I hear footsteps approaching. Leon. He says Anton and Nino are asking for me. He doesn't know why.

We go back into the ring. Nino signals for me to stand on the bar. I don't move. He and Anton come and stand either side of me.

'Okay, we'll try something else. Let yourself fall towards us. Stay perfectly straight.'

It's not difficult. They pass me back and forth from one to the other, holding me by the shoulders. Their hands feel hot to the touch.

'We'll do that again, but this time, stand with one foot in front of the other.'

More difficult.

'You see, now you're trying to balance yourself, to keep yourself from falling. It's a normal reaction. But when you're on the bar, that's exactly what you have to try and avoid.'

He places the bar on the ground. I'm supposed to stand on it, in the same way, one foot in front of the other.

'Just stand perfectly still. Okay?'

I nod. Leon stands close to me, murmuring that he's there. Anton looks straight at me. I stare at a point above his head. I feel the bar rising. My feet immediately try and find their grip. I move my arms up and down.

'Don't move!' says Nino behind me. 'Don't do anything at all!'

They hold the bar perfectly still, one metre above the ground. I stabilise myself as well as I can. My legs are shaking.

'Good. Now let yourself fall forward towards Leon, staying perfectly straight, just like you did before.'

I look down. I'm shaking even more. I try and do as Nino says, lean towards Leon. My knees start to bend, I try and control my hips but my upper body resists stubbornly. Nino tells me to stay straight as a plank, let the movement come from the hips.

I've had enough. I jump down onto the ground.

'Not bad,' says Nino. 'You really have to try and resist balancing yourself. You have to let yourself go. Focus on your hips, not your head. If you stay straight, you'll be safe. We'll keep you balanced. But if you bend at the waist, we can't do anything to catch you.'

'Very important,' Anton says. 'Safety.'

'Okay, now we'll go to shoulder level,' says Nino.

I can't speak. Anna moves closer to Leon:

'My advice is to hold on to your thighs,' she says, sympathetically. 'It makes it easier to keep still.'

Leon looks unconvinced. I watch myself getting back up on the bar.

'Imagine that you're in a swimming pool with something anchoring you to the bottom,' Leon says. 'Let your body float.'

'Or think of the air around you as having substance, like a solid object that's hard to push away,' Anna adds. 'As if you're sinking into sand.'

'Trust us,' Nino says.

With one swift movement, Anton and Nino raise me to shoulder height. Leon's and Anna's heads are level with my ankles.

'Fall towards Leon,' Nino orders.

My hands grip my thighs as hard as they can, I'm not supposed to use my legs to stabilise myself. How can you force me to trust you? I think to myself furiously. I'm hanging in the air, with no protection, almost six feet above the ground. Behind me, Nino is issuing instructions.

'You *cannot* hurt yourself. Stay straight. Fall towards Leon. The movement starts from your hips. Stay straight.'

'Stay!' Anton shouts as I bend despite myself, his features twisted in an expression I haven't seen on his face before. Fear.

I feel tears welling up in my eyes.

'Close your eyes.'

Leon's voice seems to come from somewhere far off in the distance.

I close my eyes.

Instantly, my stance feels fluid, supple, as if I'm standing on a trampoline that's not moving.

I open my eyes.

Anton and Nino are swinging me from left to right. They swing me so high that the ground is almost perpendicular to me. I let go of my thighs. I stay balanced. I try skipping from one foot to the other. Anton urges me on. I jump a bit higher. The bar follows me. I can't feel it. I watch the rows of seats moving around me, I don't even realise the bar is bringing me closer to the ground. I step off the bar and my legs give way beneath me. I'd forgotten to support myself. I start laughing. How stupid of me to fall over now.

'Not stupid at all,' Nino says. 'It's easier for a baby to learn how to stand upright than it is for an adult to learn to let go.'

He turns to face Anton:

'That was great, wasn't it?'

Anton makes a V for victory sign. He's calmed down. Leon holds out his hand to me, pulls me up sharply.

'Bravo!' Anna says.

Our building is in a great location in the centre of town. Everything is within walking distance. I like knowing that the primary school is right opposite, Thomas's office only a few minutes away. He's looking for something more spacious. His last two films did really well and now the company is making feature-length documentaries as well as dramas. One of his colleagues is conducting interviews with some of the physicists working at CERN and it made me think of you. I'm not sure exactly how it's related to physics but his report is about sports and about how we're reaching the limits of the human body and soon won't be able to improve performance through training alone. Breaking records will only be possible with the help of biomechanics.

I've been busy too. I sometimes feel that being artistic director involves juggling the skills of all the people who work at the Grand Théâtre. I'm proud of the work I've done these last few years, but it seems ages since I've actually made anything with my own hands. I probably won't renew my contract.

What about you? Our little boy talks about his holidays with you all the time. Your rail trip in the Midwest made a big impression on him. He couldn't get over the fact that it was possible to spend several days travelling through nothing but fields of wheat.

You will come and see us soon, won't you? You'd have your own room overlooking a large square. You'd only have to walk across the square and you'd be able to get to the park and the citadel, with a lake and Mont Salève a bit further away. The square is all loose gravel. It's called La Place du Cirque.

WE WATCH the training videos seated on Anton's bed with the laptop propped on the bedside table. Almost three weeks into their preparations they'd decided they were ready to attempt the four consecutive triples they were planning for the competition. The video shows Leon attaching a harness to Anna's waist and linking it to a pulley attached to the ceiling. Anton double-checks everything Leon does, commenting all the time. He makes no attempt to be subtle. This goes on for a long time. It's uncomfortable to watch, especially when he starts complaining about the double bass. He says it's really bothering him, he's fed up with being spied on by the two stupid holes on its front. The film stops. When it starts up again the double bass is concealed beneath the black cloth I've placed over it. The camera zooms in on Nino. Every time he and Anton catch Anna, he tenses his chin, a blue vein bulging in his neck, his face set in concentration. His look is more intense than Anton's. I hadn't noticed it before. As if his task is different from Anton's despite the symmetry of their positions. Anton seems to lean in, Nino to push away. Or the other way round. Anna abandons the fourth jump, twice. Anton says they'll never be ready if she carries on being scared. Or if she's still in pain.

'I'm not scared and I'm not hurting!' she shouts. 'Shit! It's the bar, it's too flexible! I'm not going high enough, I don't have time to spin.'

Her voice sounds shrill, I can't help thinking she's not being honest. That for once, she really is scared. She sits down on the ground. I zoom in on the bar. Anna's voice can be heard asking me to cut.

'What was that? Did you see that?' Leon asks. He peers closely at the screen.

The next shot is of his hands in close-up. The skin is red and wrinkled from the friction of the rope. The camera pans the length of the bar towards the bases' hands, placed one on top of the other, broad and claw-like, fingers tensed like crab pincers. Anna's feet, like hooves, laced into reinforced pumps. Then back towards the bases, their wrists. Anna. Ankles. Legs. Feet. Ankles. Wrists. The camera attempts to follow the jumps but it all happens so fast, a blur of toes that look like claws, hands that resemble talons, a body securely strapped into the safety harness, hooks at the waist, the rope sliding, the sound of clicks and pulleys, a low rumbling amplified by the microphone, echoing in the void beneath the dome of the ceiling.

I remark curtly that this is what they asked me to do, close-ups of each member of the group. The tension heightens. I wish I hadn't spoken so harshly. The only one I'm cross with is Leon. I still haven't managed to talk to him about the failure of my costumes, I don't know if he's made any progress on his end. Nino says not to worry, it's better than nothing. His kindness exasperates me. I feel even more humiliated. He moves the cursor up to the file menu. Back to the wide shot. A full body shot of Anna, panning round to take in the three of them. A tight-knit trio. He plays the film in slow motion, breaking down their movements. Anna falls jerkily. He speeds it up and slows it down, like a puppet-master. I make the excuse of needing a drink and leave.

I run into Anton and Nino on the stairs on my way back from the canteen. They've decided that the problem comes from the bar, it's too flexible for Anna, they're going to take it apart. They're bringing it down to the ring so they can do it in the daylight. I watch them as they walk away, both of them limping slightly. Anton with the left leg, Nino the right.

They place the bar on a table. Anton uses a kitchen knife to cut along the white band, revealing the three vaulting poles inside coated with a transparent, sticky material of some sort – silicone, Nino tells me. The middle section of the bar, the area where Anna lands, is reinforced with lengths of rope laid between the poles. At either end, foam pads cushion the impact on the shoulders. Nino says the foam is wearing thin, it should be changed. Anton agrees, complaining that materials today are over-priced and badly made. He scratches at the silicone with a teaspoon. Little balls of it fall away. We watch as he works. Precise gestures. The cat comes over to inspect, sniffs. Once the poles are freed, Anton unscrews the bolts that hold them together. The bolts are housed in wooden blocks inside the poles. I realise the poles are hollow. Nino cleans them with a piece of gauze soaked in alcohol. He says something to Anton, shows him one of the wooden blocks. We all lean in towards it. A hair-line crack runs for three centimetres from the spot where the bolt was screwed in. Nino straightens up:

'Good thing we've spotted it now.'

'I told you there was something wrong,' says Anna.

Anton retorts that it's nothing to do with her. He runs his finger along the crack, says he doesn't understand where it came from, he made the bar, he put it together himself.

'Is it serious?' I ask.

'It could have broken in half,' Nino says. 'But it's all right, it's just the wood. That's why it's there, so the screw doesn't touch the pole itself. It's less expensive to replace a piece of wood than all that fibreglass.'

They confer with Anna and agree to replace one of the poles with a firmer one, to avoid making too much of an adjustment this close to the performance. It's only three weeks away. Anton will talk to the Russian Athletics Federation and try to get one as soon as possible. They'll replace the white adhesive tape and buy some more foam. They've also decided to use a piece of flexible board instead of lengths of rope to create a flatter surface for Anna to land on.

Anton takes the defective pole outside. It was fine for Igor, he says. Igor was lighter. Instinctively, Leon, Nino and I all glance at Anna. She avoids our gaze, a tight smile on her lips. I feel like giving her a hug.

THE SHOPPING CENTRE is situated on the outskirts of the city, American style. Empty car park, shops with a meagre assortment of cheap clothing, sweets, discounted goods. A security guard looks us up and down. His gaze lingers on Anna. I've only ever seen her dressed in tracksuits or leotards, without make-up except for when she's performing. She's wearing a miniskirt today with thigh-high boots and a bomber jacket that accentuates her chest. I watch her as she walks, her eyes pinned to the ground. She's applied a thick layer of beige powder, her blusher is too low on her cheeks. She looks like she's puffing them out. It makes me cringe.

Anton stops in front of a bakery and suggests we get a dessert to share with the other two that evening. Leon is at the vet, Nino is busy with paperwork. Anna pouts, says she's feeling heavy after the meal last night; Anton tried making salamat, the Buryat dish, a kind of porridge made with butter, sour cream and flour. She sits down on a bench and says she'll wait for us there.

Anton dithers for ages over what to buy: stuffed cabbage leaves or some other kind of canapé. Or maybe some cakes instead. The air inside the shop smells of sugar and almond paste, the humidity makes my hair curl. There's a woman waiting behind us. The shopkeeper is becoming visibly impatient.

'Anton, what do you want?'

He's breathing more rapidly, waving his hands around. In the end he asks me to pick whatever I want, he'll wait outside. A bell tinkles as the door closes. I start filling a punnet, selecting colours that inspire me, blue, pink, green. Anna comes into the shop, moving briskly.

'Why is this taking so long?'

The other customer starts grumbling. Anna ignores her, chooses a dozen or so cakes to complete my selection.

'That many? Are you sure?'

She says they're all cakes that keep well, they get better with time, they harden up, like bread and you dip them in your tea, they're made without any butter or oil, so they go hard but not crumbly, they're the lowest-fat cakes she knows of. She leaves the shop clutching the box of cakes to her chest. I'm surprised at how animated she is. I feel like telling her that all that business about being low fat makes no sense at all, but I bite my tongue and say nothing.

She goes off with Anton to look for the materials they need for the bar. I need a few bits and pieces too. We arrange to meet in an hour's time.

I walk past a pet shop. Kittens in the window, Christmas-themed animal accessories: gold-coloured leashes, reindeer-print dog coats, rubber bell boots for horses. I remember that we're leaving for Ulan-Ude soon, in under three weeks. Leon's cat. Buck. Buck with no hair. I could make him a blanket.

One department has clothes for people as well as animals. Scarves, dresses. I flick the sequins on the scarves, swish the dresses made of nylon, polyester, acrylic, tug at the cotton-elastane blends. Mediocre quality. I've been meaning to look for something to cover up my psoriasis. A member of staff comes over to talk to me. Her perfume makes my nose itch. Her face is caked in powder, I feel like reaching out and brushing it off. She says something to me that I don't understand. She wraps a coat round my shoulders and turns me towards a mirror. I make the mistake of smiling. The coat goes down to my ankles. The fake fur feels soft but it still irritates my neck. She says it suits me, places a beaver fur hat on my head and turns to rummage through the gloves. She lingers over a pair with a crocodile motif then starts sifting through the scarves. I'm the only customer here, she's in no hurry to move on. I want to tell her that I'm not interested in any of it, all I'm looking for is something to cover the scabbing that's spreading over the back of my neck. I end up buying a reindeer-print scarf.

WE MEET UP with Nino in the courtyard outside the circus. Beers, crisps and gherkins on the table, blankets on the chairs. Leon isn't back yet. The wind feels surprisingly warm for late November. Anton goes backstage to find a saw for the snowboard he's bought to make a flat surface for Anna to land on. Nino teases him about the Superman motif on it.

'He didn't look very hard,' Anna says. 'He saw it in the window. On sale.'

Anton says something to her, defending his choice. I can understand some of what he's saying, he's talking about what's wrong with shops today, he says there's too much choice, there weren't so many options when he was young, you could always rely on the quality.

Anna opens a beer, wraps herself in a blanket. She pulls off her boots and rubs her feet. The heels of her boots are completely worn down. I sit down, facing the water, nibble on some crisps. Military vessels ply back and forth under the great bridge. I screw up my eyes. It's late afternoon, the light is fading, becoming more bleached out as the month progresses. In Europe, the light turns yellow; here, it has a translucent quality. Solid objects seem to lose density, matter becomes brittle, cracks appear – stone, glass, shale, trees. Dry cold.

Nino brings up the subject of our trip. He's been doing some research. We need to make reservations for the train. Two days and nights, via Khabarovsk. As the crow flies, it would be shorter to cross into China and take the Trans-Manchurian Railway as far as Chita, then pick up the Trans-Siberian. But getting visas is complicated, we'd have to go to Moscow. And flying isn't an option, Anton and Nino won't even consider it. They're afraid of damaging the bar. Nino plans to meet up with his family after the festival; they're on tour in the Frankfurt area for the Christmas season. Anton is meeting his family in Irkutsk, Anna in Kyiv. Leon is going with Nino. He has a brother in Canada who is in prison for repeated shoplifting. Their parents live in a closed community. I didn't know any of this, I feel slighted. I opened up to him about myself the day we went to Russky Island but he hasn't said anything at all to me about his family.

'What about you, Nathalie?' Nino asks.

I haven't really thought about it, I say. I bought a one-way ticket to come here, I wanted to keep my options open as long as possible. Nino says there's an airport near Ulan-Ude.

'I don't want to fly,' I say. 'I'd rather go to Moscow by train. I know it's a long journey but I don't mind.'

Anna opens a second beer. Nino gives her a disapproving look. I stiffen in response. I start to explain that I hate flying, I get it from my father, he's completely phobic about it.

'It's ridiculous,' I say. 'He spent years flying from one lab to another with no problem at all, and then suddenly he couldn't do it unless he knocked himself out with sleeping pills. Ever since then, he's gone by ship whenever he can. He hasn't been over to see me for two years, the journey takes too long. He doesn't drive but I do. I've driven him all over Europe.'

I stop to take a sip of beer before explaining that my father is mad about train travel. He takes the train whenever he can. It's not so easy in the US, the railways aren't as good there.

'He's in Massachusetts,' I add. 'He plans to stay there for a while.'

I put the bottle back on the table and realise that I've been drinking Anna's beer. I haven't eaten. I can't handle alcohol. I'm afraid of what I might say. I ask if they'd mind if I told them a story and launch into an anecdote about when I first arrived in Chicago.

'I was having a hard time adjusting to school. I didn't speak any English. Olga spoke French to me in Vladivostok, my father asked her to, she'd taught it at university. She was retired – I think I've already told you that. He'd bought me a subscription to a French magazine for children that she used to read to me. I can remember one story about a little Mongolian girl of my age who was training for a traditional horse race. It's funny that we're going to be in Ulan-Ude soon . . .'

'Ulan-Ude is in Russia,' Anna says, interrupting me.

'I know,' I say. 'But it's not far from Mongolia. Anyway, I was crazy about horses, my dad knew I was. He arranged a surprise for me on the first day of the holidays.

I went to sleep in my bed in Chicago and when I woke up, I was in a stable somewhere in the countryside.'

Anna stares at me. I can see she's curious. She looks annoyed with herself for wanting to hear more. Then, she says:

'You go to sleep in your own bed and you wake up lying on straw that stinks to high heaven. And you're actually dumb enough not to notice anything happening in between?'

'That's just it,' I reply smugly. 'He wanted it to be a surprise for me, so he gave me a sleeping pill to make sure I didn't wake up before we got there.'

'Brilliant!' Nino exclaims.

He turns to Anna:

'Your family have horses, don't they?'

'He's responsible for a kid and he drugs her up with prescription pills?'

'I think it's cool. Why don't you tell us a story for once?'

'Like what?'

'I dunno. Something original, whatever.'

She cracks open her third beer.

'You shouldn't have any more,' Nino says.

'Tomorrow's a day off.'

'Well, not exactly.'

She stares out at the fence and takes a long draught of beer. She says he's naïve. Nino glances at me, looks over at Anton who's busy sawing.

'He's the one who's naïve,' he says with forced cheeriness.

'What?' Anton says without looking up.

'I'm going to tell them about how I messed up,' Nino says. He turns to face me and continues:

'It's true, I really screwed up with alcohol. I was drinking after shows, to decompress. I started when I was around fifteen. Anton was horribly strict about it. He bribed me by saying he'd stop training me if I carried on drinking. He started hovering over me all the time to check up on me. Sometimes he wouldn't leave me alone until I actually went to sleep. He even said I couldn't go to my dad's fiftieth birthday celebration because he wouldn't be able to go with me. It was the day before our first performance with Igor.'

Anna spins round in her chair.

'What did you do?' she asks.

'I went to the party, what do you think?'

I try injecting a bit of humour.

'So? Did you earn his trust?'

'What did he say?' Anna persists.

When Nino answers, I have the feeling he's no longer talking just to her.

'He asked me if I was up to it. Just as we were going on.'

'Yeah, but what about you? How did it make you feel? What did you do? Truthfully?'

Nino turns to Anton, who says he doesn't want to hear any more about it, they won the first prize, that's all that counts. Nino laughs. He's lucky to be able to work with someone like Anton, he says. In spite of everything.

'What about you?' I ask Anton.

'Yeah, why don't you tell us something interesting?' Nino adds.

Anton grumbles. We press him further. He thinks for a long time and finally spits out a few words.

'He did his military service as a cook in a submarine in the Soviet era,' Nino says, translating.

'And? What did he cook?'

Anton mumbles something in response.

'He can't say.'

'Why not?'

Anton shakes his head.

'He says he's not allowed to reveal military secrets.'

I start to laugh but end up hiccoughing instead. Anton announces, deadpan, that before we leave for Ulan-Ude, once we're all ready to go, he plans to take us out to a restaurant. He's found one that's really smart, traditional. He won't tell us which one. He wants it to be a surprise.

Anna eats from the box of cakes on her lap, scooping up crumbs and cream with the tip of her finger and licking it carefully. I've never seen her eating like this before. She's downed three beers and eaten all the cakes. She wipes her mouth. Says she's sorry, she was hungry.

Anton has finished what he was working on. He shows us the piece of wood, the illustrated side facing towards us. Nino hoots with laughter. Anton turns it over and sees that he's cut out a square right in the middle of Superman's trunks.

'I love it!' Nino says, still laughing. He turns to Anna and adds, 'Can you imagine the reaction if the audience could see that?'

She stands up briskly. Her skirt is all creased. It's getting dark. An electric cable creaks. We go back inside. Anna wraps the blanket tightly around her shoulders. Her silhouette makes me think of a peasant woman in a painting. I start to shiver, I feel annoyed with the day. For being so warm, for failing to fulfil its promise.

LATER THAT EVENING, I notice a faint glow at the end of the corridor. The bathroom door is open. I hurry towards it – the hall light only comes on for a few moments. I usually try to get there before Anna.

Outside the door, I stop.

Anna is crouched, naked, her back turned towards me. I can see the muscles around her spine all the way down to her hips, which look wider because of her squatting position. She seems to have filled out since I took her measurements. Her skin is startlingly white. She gathers up fragments of a jar that's fallen to the ground, scrapes the body lotion, lumpy with pieces of broken glass, from the floor and plops it all into the mug where she usually keeps her toothbrush. Her bare body looks rigid with cold, her shoulders hunched. She's completely still, only her forearms move. Shards of glass are spattered far and wide. She leans over and as she kneels something crunches beneath her knees.

I wait by the door until she disappears into the shower. She emerges in a cloud of steam, dressed in an oversized jumper emblazoned with the image of a rock band. I'm already in my pyjamas. We brush our teeth in front of the mirror. I try not to stare at her knees, reddened from the tiny cuts. Anna spits into the sink. Now and then, an animal smell, exactly like the one backstage, wafts into the room through the fan. Anna looks up, says the same thing happens in zoos. The cages still smell even after the animals have died, a testament to their lives spent in captivity. She sees me staring at the mug filled with lotion and broken glass:

'It'd make a great face mask, don't you think?'

She mimes sticking her finger into it and spreading the cream over her face.

'To peel off all those scraps of dead skin?'

I give her an enquiring look. She laughs.

'I'm kidding,' she says, a hint of warmth in her voice.

She sets the mug full of broken glass aside to throw it away. Not much gets recycled here. Half smiling, she tells me to put on a jacket.

'Come on,' she says. 'I've got something I want to show you.'

Backstage, Anna draws aside a velvet drape, revealing a steel double door. She pushes it open. A staircase leads down to the basement. The same acrid smell drifts up.

'How did you know about this?'

'I spotted it when I first arrived but I didn't want to go down there alone.'

'No wonder,' I say.

I go first, lighting the way with my phone torch.

'Did you say something?' she asks, her voice echoing in the cavernous space. The steps get wetter as we descend.

'We must be down at sea level,' I say when I reach the bottom.

We're in a passageway. The ground underfoot is uneven: concrete slabs, barely discernible in the dim light, with patches of mud and straw that muffle the sound of our footsteps. Panels of metal to our right and left.

'Cages,' Anna whispers behind me.

I shine my torch on them. Cages strewn with a thin bed of straw. We follow the curve of the passageway and arrive at a point where it forks. The darkness lifts a little. Light from the lamppost filters in through a grille in the ceiling. The vents in the courtyard. I thought they were sewage pipes. Warm air blows in from ventilation holes, the smell seems to emanate from them. We give them a wide berth. I touch the wall. It feels damp and springy, like a piece of steak. The walls are lined with rubber.

'For the animals,' Anna says. 'To stop them hurting themselves if they panicked and banged into the walls. They had to come through here to get to the ring. The sand is for the iron horseshoes.'

I can't see any cages in this part of the tunnel, only stalls. Anna walks on ahead, points out the feeding troughs. She thinks this was probably only a passageway, she can tell from the size of the troughs. The horses couldn't have been kept down here for long periods, they need space to turn around and lie down. She runs her hand along a cord attached to the rail, says it's there for protection too. The bridle, or the halter, needs to be tethered to something the horse can pull out if it rears up or steps back suddenly. It could break its neck other-wise. She speaks slowly, choosing her words carefully, in perfect English. I thank her for making the effort. She looks up. I apologise for not being able to speak Russian. I can just about read the Cyrillic alphabet now, but I get confused by the letter 'p'. I know it's meant to be pronounced like an 'r', but I keep thinking of it as 'p'. The Russian word for restaurant for example. I can't help reading as it as 'pectopan'. I'd like to take a class. I thought of asking Leon to teach me. After all, he is a teacher, but I don't want to cause any inconvenience.

'Why bother? You're not here for very long.'

'That's true.'

Out of the blue I start telling her about the only time I ever rode a horse.

'It was in the US. The horse was walking quickly, trotting almost, it was making a weird noise on the tarmac, I could feel myself being bounced rhythmically up and down, I started laughing from the stress of it, the instructor kept shouting at me to stay at the rear of the group but I couldn't control the horse and I was out in front of everyone else, laughing like an idiot, and the more she shouted at me, the more frightened I became and the more I laughed. I finally ended up level with her, the horse started galloping in place, so I followed her instructions and drew one rein out to the side to make the horse turn, I was trying to think of everything she'd said to us before we set out on the ride, you have to keep your hands and your heels low down, back straight, squeeze with your legs, look straight ahead, that's what I was trying to do, pulling the rein out sideways the whole time, and the horse was going in ever decreasing circles until it was spinning around like a dog trying to bite its own tail. When it finally stopped, it was sweating like mad. You should have seen how hard it was breathing, my legs were actually being lifted up off the horse's back. It looked like it couldn't take another step. The one and only time in my life I've ever been on a horse. And then when it stopped, I managed to fall off!'

'Why? If the horse had stopped moving?'

'That's the most ridiculous thing about it! Sorry, I hadn't quite finished the story. I just slid off. Literally. I let myself drop to the ground. As if it was the logical conclusion to what had just happened. I think I thought it was a bit like the horse wanted to let me know that I wasn't meant to be riding it. It's not a big deal, but at the time, it did upset me, because I'd read so many books about horses and I was convinced it was all going to be fine. My father too. I could see how disappointed he was.'

'Is he coming to see you in Ulan-Ude?' Anna asks.

'We haven't seen each other for two years. I'd be surprised if he showed up, all the way out in Siberia. I haven't even told him I'm here.'

'Are things that bad between you?'

I look at her, taken aback.

'No, I told you! He doesn't fly!'

'He could make the effort.'

'He does the best he can. If I was going over there, he'd pay for all my tickets.'

I show her a picture on my phone. Part of a wall, covered with posters for Thomas's film, press cuttings.

'He sent me this yesterday. His office.'

'And that? What's that?' she says, blowing up part of the picture.

'Screenshots of characters wearing my costumes. I sent him the film. He blew it up too much. You can see the pixels.'

I scroll through two, three more pictures, similar to the first one.

'When he does that, it makes me want to screw everything up. Just to show him I'm light-years away from what he imagines.'

'What is it you want him to believe? If you keep lying to him?' Anna counters.

I look straight at her. I've never lied. He just doesn't know where I am, that's different.

'We get on perfectly well,' I say, becoming increasingly annoyed. 'We just don't really know each other, that's all.'

'You don't give him any way to get to know you,' she says.

I don't respond. I know we have more to say but neither of us wants to break the silence.

'And what about you?' I ask eventually. 'What about your family?'

She says her father will be there. For the first time. He's never seen her performing as a flyer. He never even came during the trampoline days. From the way she says it, I have a feeling she's been wanting to get this off her chest for a long time.

'Well, he'll have a whole posse of clients with him,' she adds hastily. 'And he's coming because Ulan-Ude is a big festival. He trades racehorses. Pure-bred Arabians. You know? Not like your family at all, that's for sure. I can't stand animals. Seriously. I loathe horses. His stud farm is like a luxury hotel. When he sells a horse, he delivers it by plane and goes with it himself to personally guarantee its pedigree. Talk about over the top!'

She sits down on the straw, wraps her arms around her knees:

'I don't know why I'm telling you this. I don't even care about any of it. I just hope he won't be with my mother. She'll be all over him. And he's sleeping with someone else. She's the same age as me. I don't know what disgusts me the most. My father's gross, he's so fat he can't even put his own socks on any more. My mother does it for him. Well, she did when I was there. I don't know about now.'

I crouch down beside her, making sure I don't touch either the wall or the floor.

'Anna, this is your mother and father you're talking about.'

'Obviously, I take after him, you can see that. He's always said I was too fat for his thoroughbred horses. He said if I rode one I'd break its back.'

She laughs bitterly.

'He told me he'd have raised Soviet draught horses if he'd known I was going to turn out so chunky. The ones with the flaxen mane and huge thighs.'

She slaps herself on the thigh. I listen to the sound echoing in the silence. I say timidly that I don't think she'd have become a champion trampolinist at such a young age if she was that fat. She says she doesn't need any sanctimonious lecturing from me.

Sounds from the courtyard drift down to us through the ventilation grille. Leon and Nino talking.

'Do you think they've heard us?' Anna murmurs.

It's hard to make out what they're saying through the noise of the fan. We listen intently. They're speaking Russian, talking about the cat, Anna says. Leon had to wait for test results, that's why he's so late back. There's something seriously wrong, the vet isn't quite sure what. Leon's not sure he'll be able to come to Ulan-Ude with us. Anna's expression darkens. My presence is less important than Leon's, I suggest. I could stay behind here instead of him.

'Please don't bullshit me,' she says, switching to English again. 'It's not as if the cat's actually died.'

'His name is Buck,' I say.

She glares at me. The voices recede into the distance. Then silence.

Anna sighs. She says Leon gets too attached. I ask her if there's ever been anything between them.

'With Leon?'

She shakes her head, says he's besotted with his tight-rope walker anyway.

'What's she like?'

Anna thinks for a moment.

'Hard work.'

'What do you mean?'

She shoots me a sidelong glance. I feel myself blushing.

'Control freak. Makes sense for someone who walks on a highwire. That's probably the reason Leon became such a good circus technician.'

She sighs:

'How can you be responsible for the safety of someone you love that much? You're there during training, but during the performance there's nothing you can do. She's out there on her own on the highwire. You can always run up and climb the tower on the other side to be closer to her, but you're waiting for her to get to you, you can't do anything except watch her putting one foot in front of the other on a wire. I don't know how he can stand it.'

I visualise Anna, up in space, seven metres high in the air.

'And anyway,' she adds, 'I'm getting married. We're planning to do it next year.'

She says she's known him since they were children. He's a doctor in Kyiv, they don't see each other very much, he was the one who wanted to get married, she's excited about it but she's a bit worried that it will make him even more jealous, he gives her a hard time about that.

The idea of marriage seems so remote to me in my own life, I can't help asking her if she's really going to get married. She says she doesn't have much choice.

'No one's forcing you to,' I say indignantly.

She looks at me:

'When I was on the trampoline, everyone was always telling me how young I was to be doing what I did. No one ever says that to me any more.'

I confess to her that I've sometimes thought that Anton is hard on her during training. She shrugs. He's tougher with Nino. She worries about them. Anton is nearly sixty-five years old. He goes on and on doing Russian bar but he'd be better off helping Nino find a new partner, someone younger. He knows Nino will never give up on him. Then she adds angrily:

'You know how much that bar weighs when I land? One day, Anton won't be able to hold it for long enough. Imagine if he collapses, if he doesn't realise that his strength is deserting him. How do you know when you've got to the point where you have to stop doing the thing you've done all your life?'

'Surely he'll know, won't he? With all the experience he has.'

'You only get old once.'

She twists a piece of straw.

'Maybe with Igor, they'd have made it, got to the very top.'

She pauses for a moment and then says:

'You know, they really are incredibly strong. I'm not saying this because . . .'

Her voice cracks again.

'Because what?'

'Oh, nothing.'

I'd like to be able to tell her that I have a lot of admiration for her. Instead, I say something about feeling half the time that I don't know what I'm doing either.

'Is that why you always take on too much?'

She stands up.

We go back upstairs covered in dust. When we get to the door backstage, just as we're about to go our separate ways, she stops. Turning to me, she says:

'Don't worry, we're going to be just fine. The routine, I mean. We'll master it. I wouldn't have said any of this otherwise.'

BEFORE I GO to bed I make my way back to the canteen. It smells of alcohol, disinfectant. I feel tipsy even though I didn't have very much to drink. I boil some water. Behind me, between the two chairs, the bar, white adhesive tape hanging down on either side. Flecks of silicone on the tiled floor. I suppress the urge to clean it up. Like Anna said, I try and do too much. It's true.

I think about my father. I haven't seen him for two years. What does he look like now? My parents had me quite late, they were already in their forties. My only memory of my mother is of a hospital. A blanket, scratchy and blindingly white, a floor like the one here, tiled in green. My mother's face covered with an oxygen mask that amplifies the sound of her breathing. As if the whole room is breathing through her. The windows kept firmly shut, the air stagnating, becoming heavier. Liquid drips from a plastic pouch into her body. A needle inserted into the back of her hand provides her nourishment. My father and I sleep in her room during the last days, in temporary beds. I watch their chests rising and falling, check constantly to make sure they're still moving. After her death, my father lost weight, his angular frame made starker by his shaved head. His hands were always ice cold. I told him he should let his hair grow, it would keep him warmer. He came home from work one day and stood next to me, staring at himself in the mirror for a long time. He put his razor away after that. One week later, his head was covered in grey. His tall frame seemed even thinner to me, he looked older too. I wished I hadn't said anything.

THE NEW POLE is delivered the next day. As always, Anton takes command of the proceedings. He peels back the protective film, places the new pole between the two old ones, then asks me to shine my phone light on it while Anna and Nino squeeze the poles together. I do as he asks, feeling annoyed at Leon for not being there. It feels like an affront to me. I hardly ever see him any more. I don't understand how he can disappear like this when Ulan-Ude is less than three weeks away. I still don't know what I should do for costumes, he hasn't suggested a choreography. I feel like I'm the only one who's at all concerned about it.

'What's Leon doing?' I ask.

Nino says he saw him earlier that morning, he was down by the water. Eating an ice cream.

'An ice cream?'

'Nathalie, the light!' Anna says.

I look down, turn my phone light back on. Anton uses a tube of silicone to seal the gaps. Anna blows air at it with a hairdryer. Anton marks the mid-point of the bar, attaches the piece of wood he cut out from the snowboard and secures it with my super-strength glue. He renews the foam at the ends. Nino explains that it has to be just right, not too thin and definitely not too thick. That would reduce the precision of their contact with the bar. He says thank you, I can turn off my light. He and Anton start wrapping the bar with adhesive tape. Anna checks to make sure there are no creases. I hover, making a show of how closely I'm watching. There's not much else I can do.

Two hours later, the silicone has dried and they go into the ring to try out the bar. Instead of sitting in the front row as I usually do, I go and sit high up at the back. Just at that moment, Leon appears. He comes over and seats himself next to me, the sleeves of his jumper rolled up. I can smell the wind on him.

'Have they finished already?' he asks.

'You can see for yourself.'

I grope nervously in my pockets and find a Sugarsea sweet that's been in there for three weeks. It's survived being put through the wash.

'Do you want it?' I ask Leon.

He declines. I try and peel off the wrapping. It's stuck.

'You shouldn't eat that,' he says. 'It's past its best-before date.'

'You're the one who gave it to me.'

'I don't think so.'

'You filled up the baskets for the audience.'

'Ah. Well, that's different.'

I look straight at him.

'It's fine to eat,' he says. 'But it's past its best-before date.'

I stuff the sweet into my mouth. Acrid, sugary taste, then salt, with a hint of seaweed. It dissolves into tiny pieces.

'Be careful,' Nino shouts. 'It's firmer.'

Anna nods. She's mounted the bar. Anton and Nino bend their knees more deeply, steady themselves.

'Will they have enough time to get used to the new bar?' I wonder out loud.

'I hope so,' Leon mutters.

I watch as Anna rebounds higher than I've ever seen her do before, her jump powerful and perfectly executed. She adjusts her balance as she lands, arms fluttering like a hummingbird's wings. She rises again and again, each leap more perilous than the last until finally she steps off the bar, satisfied.

'Now it's good,' she declares.

LEON DISAPPEARED just after the end of the session. I saw him going up to the canteen. I've decided I must speak to him. I find him with the cat, who has spent all his time since the visit to the vet under a radiator, wrapped in a blanket. Leon crushes pills into a spoonful of yoghurt and offers it to Buck on the palm of his hand.

'He keeps vomiting,' Leon says as I kneel down next to them. 'He's been like this for the past two days.'

He points to the bag of cat biscuits open beside us. 'He won't eat them,' he says. 'I can't say I blame him. They smell foul, those things.'

The cat places a paw in Leon's hand and starts to lick.

'Why is he doing that?' I ask.

'I taught him to do tricks when he was little.'

I run my fingers lightly over the ailing creature's haunches, his hairless back.

'What's wrong with his skin?'

'Fleas. He was infested. I had to shave off all his fur. It's never really grown back. I found him on the street.'

A spasm shakes the cat, he tries to sit up, preparing to vomit. Nothing. He lies back down. Leon whispers something soothing to him, one hand on his abdomen. I do my best to be reassuring, say we can try again tomorrow. He nods, replaces the lid on the pot of yoghurt, opens the fridge door and points to a jar of something white and lumpy suspended in yellow liquid.

'What's that stuff?' I ask.

'Kefir,' he says. I take the yoghurt pot out of his hands and put it in the bin – it's probably contaminated with cat germs. 'Anton made it yesterday. We have to wait for it to ferment.'

'Is that new?' he says, pointing at my reindeer scarf.

'No,' I lie.

'Where have the others got to?'

'I haven't a clue.'

'What about you? What are you doing here?'

Nervously, I tell him I'd like to do some work, we've only got two weeks left, I need him to give me some guidance. He says he knows. He's really sorry. He doesn't have enough time either. Things haven't been easy for him. It's the first time he's directed a group as high-profile as these three. He needs to have time alone to mull things over. He's been thinking about my father's job. And the costumes I showed them on my phone the day after I arrived.

'You want me to wrap Anna in cellophane?' I say incredulously. 'Give her shoes made of lead?'

'I liked your costumes,' he says, ignoring my last remark. 'Not that I understood what you were trying to say with your film.'

'It's not my film.'

He gives me a weary look, and says I have to take some ownership of it. I try and come up with something to say in response. A cutting remark.

'So, what should the story be?' I ask eventually.

'Something simple,' he says.

'Come with me,' he adds, walking towards his bedroom.

His room is no bigger than Anton's. It looks lived in. Piles of books and DVDs on the floor, plants on the windowsill. The ceiling is plastered with album covers of all sizes, creating an illusion of depth. Leon glances at my outfit: dungarees, roll-neck jumper. He lies on the floor, invites me to do the same. Or I could lie on the bed if I prefer. I stretch out beside him, intrigued. I tease him about his posters of superhero films, I think of them as children's films. Unperturbed, he starts explaining to me that if you direct your gaze upwards, your brain will tend towards positive emotions.

'That's probably why very tall people are often pessimistic. They're always looking down. Or else it's genetic, something to do with the gene for being tall.'

'Why are you telling me all this?'

'Just because.'

I look up at the pictures pinned to the ceiling. A cow in a field of deep green grass, a baby swimming, headlines in Russian, photos of rockets, psychedelic colours. He puts on some music, I don't recognise any of it except that most of it seems to be from the 1980s. Leon turns and faces me. I can feel his breath as he says:

'Imagine the act is happening in space. Weightless. A single jump would be enough to propel Anna towards infinity.'

Thomas's film had given him the idea of Anna as a heavenly body, with the bar itself and the two bases as the planet around which she gravitates.

'Yes, but what would it be *about*?' I insist.

He says we don't have to tell a story, if that's what I mean. There doesn't have to be a narrative. If we succeeded in suggesting the idea of the body submitting to the pull of gravity, that would be enough.

'And the act would be called *Gravity*? Like something out of Spielberg?' I say, doing my best to sound light-hearted in a desperate effort to cover up my embarrassment at feeling his face so close to mine.

'Or *Star Wars*.'

We both laugh. Warming to the joke, we start poking fun at super-hero films, how implausible they are. I've always wondered about the costumes, what kind of fabrics they use. They seem to have an infinite capacity to stretch, until they come into contact with the enemy and then they rip. Maybe they should wear nothing at all, Leon says. No one gives it a second thought when some characters are naked. Babar, for example, before he puts on a suit, or the Barbapapas.

I've never heard of them. He googles them, shows me an image of a family of brightly coloured creatures.

'More your age group than mine,' he says. I can't tell if he's joking. One way or the other there's suddenly more of a distance between us.

I turn my mind back to the costumes. The most important thing for Anna is to be comfortable. Her costume must allow her to move freely without restricting her at all. A second skin that hugs her but doesn't cling. I scan the ceiling, wondering if there is a way of showing a body without it actually being visible. One of the album covers catches my attention. A man standing in a rocky plain, his back turned, wearing an outfit covered with illuminated bulbs, like pears sprouting from his body. To his right, a lake. Across from him, another man outlined on the horizon, a cloud of indeterminate objects suspended in the air around him, a flock of birds in flight perhaps.

Leon gets up from the floor and seats himself at the small table, a notebook open in front of him. I sit up, cross-legged. A cloud of dust rises. Leon writes, staring off into space from time to time, one foot resting on the other knee. I stand up.

'Right, I'm off to do some work.'

Leon nods but says nothing.

An image is beginning to take shape in my mind. Anna's skin, encrusted with shards of glass. Light glinting off the glass. All we see are the traces of her flight through the air. Gravity pulling her back down. Her shadow, then a flash. I begin to visualise a costume of lights. I set out my materials around the caravan. I want to be able to work undisturbed. I hang the big scissors on the hook of the hanger holding the panther costume. I look at the marks the scissor's metal loops leave on my fingers and thumb. The fine blades, almost as long as my forearms. They feel like an extension of my fingers. I know their exact weight. How do you experience weight in flight? Anna is leaping from a new bar. The almost imperceptible difference of rigidity allows her to increase the height of her jumps by at least a metre. Propulsion, suspension point, return to earth. It occurs to me that my materials can have an impact on their act too. Smoothing out the skin, tapering the body, enabling it to rise more quickly and to a greater height. And at the same time, accelerating the fall.

From the window, you could look out on all those people hurrying by, heads bowed against the wind. You'd watch them scurrying along, dressed in their trench coats, on their way to catch their tram to the station or perhaps to France. I didn't notice the vans in the square at first yesterday. Lots of them, unloading their contents there, in the square. It took all afternoon. They started from the middle and worked outwards, steel poles rising, spools of cables unwinding, spilling out their guts, anchoring everything to the ground. And just before nightfall, with a single movement, the big top was raised. Blue, studded with stars. 'Starlight' written in big letters over the ticket booths.

The last time I went to the circus was the year I went back to Russia. The setting was very different. In Eastern Siberia, on the steppes of Buryatia. Even the horse droppings froze instantly. I can still see them in the ring, the friends I worked with. I can see their faces, their strange smiles. In the circus, you become attached, whatever happens.

EARLY DECEMBER. The cold set in one night. The thermometer has stalled. Hazy sunlight shrouds the shoreline. We decide to heat only the canteen and the bedrooms we are using; the heating bill is charged to us. A gentle warmth gathers in the glass dome. Nino sets up a heater in the caravan, with the aid of a long cable plugged in backstage. At night, the wind howls. We keep the windows closed, it's too cold to open them. Damp takes hold in the bathrooms. Nothing dries. Mildew blooms between the tiles. One morning I find myself thinking how beautiful it looks, until I remember it's nothing more than mould suffocating the walls. I press on it, half expecting it to come away on my fingers.

The costumes are ready for fitting. For the men, some-thing subdued. A plain velour outfit, no headdress. Black leather slippers. And from wrist to neck, a band of light, to give the illusion of extending the bar in Anna's wake. Anna, the moon, silvery light. Lycra bodysuit. Leon found some strings of LED lights for me. They were sent from Moscow. I stitch them from the collar to the ankles taking care not to tear the fabric. Every stitch must be reinforced. It takes forever. A costume studded with lights. I work late into the night. The group were excited about the new theme. During the day, I black out the windows of the caravan to test the effect. The costumes are draped all over the room, hanging up in the windows, on the door, over the back of my chair, on my bed. I don't always clean them after they've been worn. The room is full of their smell. Anton's is reminiscent of old wood in a cellar, Nino's smells of berries, with a sour tang of cigarette smoke, Anna's of moisturiser. Sweat. I repeat words to myself as I work. Attraction. Gravity. Moving through the atmosphere, shooting towards Earth. Pulsing. Anna, a comet, an asteroid, stardust. Black hole. An act performed in darkness. Four dangerous triple jumps. With Leon's help, they create a simple choreog-raphy. The first two jumps will be performed in quick succession in tuck position, the next two without the tuck, the final one ending with a twist.

I've built up a little stock of Sugarsea sweets. I press the wrappers to my lips, wait for them to dissolve and entertain myself trying to anticipate the exact moment when the sugar will flood my mouth and I'll start to gag. Leon has decided on the music. Very bass-heavy. It makes my head throb. I hear it and feel my stomach clench. Anton worries about the technical aspects, he's concerned about our idea of performing in semi-darkness with costumes studded with lightbulbs. He says the trio need to be able to see properly, the ceiling has to be clearly visible for them to be able to situate things in space, especially under an unfamiliar big top. Leon and I reassure him, we'll do everything possible to keep them safe, the only danger will come from the jumps themselves. Leon brings me cups of tea, makes an effort to communicate better. I have a vision of him back in his room. He's the only one I haven't taken measurements for, the only one whose skin I haven't touched, whose smell I can't identify. And I came so close to him, my face almost touching his.

Our food shopping and meals are becoming more and more chaotic. Whenever I open the fridge, the sight of all that pickled, acidic food – gherkins, cucumbers, lemons, yoghurt – gives me the chills. But not Anna's aerosol whipped cream – all that fat. The pots of yoghurt are still organised by colour. We have a tacit agreement that everyone seems to respect. I eat them when no one else is around, I feel embarrassed about it, I don't know if they realise I'm the one who started organising them like this.

My cooking has improved. Thomas used to make a delicious cauliflower soup. I wanted to ask him for the recipe. I hesitated at first but when I did ask, he messaged me back straight away. He didn't seem to mind at all. I cut up the cauliflower, chop the onion. The cooking pot is huge, I could almost plunge my whole head and shoulders into it. I pour in some water, toss in the cauliflower. Anton watches what I'm doing, between working on his wooden boxes. He has them scattered all over the corridor, there isn't enough space for all of them in his room. Their construction is becoming more rudimentary, when he runs out of wood he uses cardboard and wraps it in foil. Some of them look more like boats than boxes. He says he's behind schedule. He has to finish them before winter sets in because it's now that birds are building up stocks of food. Steam escapes from the pot. I open the window. Just at that moment, a message from Thomas comes in: *So? How is it?* I lift the lid. The cauliflower florets bump up against each other in the boiling water. I lower the heat to calm them a little. They simmer, shaking gently from time to time. I send a picture with the caption: *Brains bubbling with ideas.*

The meal is a success. Afterwards, Anton pats his stomach and says he misses France.

'Why?' I ask, suppressing a smile. 'What do you miss about it?'

'I was in Nice. I liked weather. Nice weather.'

I picture him in a 1930s setting, cycling along the shoreline, with sunglasses and a striped sailor top. I chuckle to myself at the absurdity of the image.

We watch videos of other competitors. They know all of them and make comparisons. Sometimes they're happy about something they see – a trapeze artist they think has lowered the standard. I'm getting better at videoing their training sessions. They've started rehearsing in the evenings. They leave the bar in the caravan, practise the routine with bare feet, do group exercises to build trust, pass an imaginary ball between them. Their hands move rapidly. They walk up and down with their eyes closed, brush past each other, spring back if they come into contact, like atoms splitting apart. Meanwhile, the imaginary ball has bounced off and landed in the risers. No one goes to retrieve it. They repeat the exercise later, with music, forcing themselves to follow Leon's instruction to smile. I like seeing Nino and Anna smiling like this. With Anton, it makes me feel sad. He looks like an overgrown child. And I can't stand the music. It doesn't make any sense to me. It has nothing to do with the story I've imagined for them. Sometimes Leon stops giving directions and sits by the side of the ring, chin propped in one hand, staring at a point somewhere in the risers. I stop filming. I gaze at this man lost in a reverie I cannot penetrate. Pausing from my work allows me to feel that I'm part of that reverie.

THIS HARMONY is shattered one Sunday morning as we are tidying up loose ends in the canteen after breakfast. The sun hangs in mist, a clearly defined circle. The ocean is hidden from view. I've opened a window to let in some air. The cold plays havoc with my hair. We're leaving in a week. Yesterday Anna came close to perfecting the routine. A slight hesitation just before the final jump stopped her from attempting it. They decide on an alternative strategy as a back-up in case something like this happens on the night. They'd be happy with what they have already mastered, four triples but landing on the ground between two of them. This alone would confirm

Anna's status among the very best. Leon and I are given the task of going to pick up the train tickets. We've just decided on this when a bird crashes into a windowpane. It flies off again erratically and then floats in through the open window and lands under the table at our feet. We gaze at it, trying to take in what has happened. Buck rises to his feet beneath his blanket. Anton hurls a spoon in his direction. The spoon lands a few centimetres from the cat's head. He backs off.

'Are you out of your mind?' Leon says.

Anton walks over to the cat and strokes him rather stiffly before kneeling beside the bird. Its eyes are darting about in panic, its wings at an awkward angle. They seem too large for its body. The bird is small and black, the sheen on its feathers almost reptilian in aspect. I've never seen a bird at such close quarters. Its wide-eyed stare unsettles me. Leon thinks it's a swift. He says you often see them around here. You can recognise them from their oversized wings and legs so delicate they can't take flight from the ground. They need a high point to launch themselves from. Some of them spend their whole lives on the wing, never landing and sleeping ten kilometres high in the air.

'If you see one at ground level, it means it has a problem,' Nino says.

I look up towards the dome. The metal bars that meet at the apex look like the mouth of a carnivorous plant.

'Is it still alive?' Anna asks.

The body seems so small in Anton's hands. He turns it over. Liquid seeps from its belly and drips onto the floor.

'It's disgusting,' she says. 'You should have gloves on.'

Nino says we should start by cleaning up the mess. Anton takes the dead bird away, he wants to bury it behind the fence, in the sand. Leon rubs the floor with a rag then points out another mark, on the window, on the other side of the glass, out of reach. The rain can wash that away, he says. When though? I wonder. It hasn't rained at all since I've been here.

THE NEXT DAY, thirty-eight days after I arrived, Anna becomes the first woman in the world to execute four perilous triple jumps in a row landing only on the bar between jumps.

A TREE STANDS in the station concourse, an evergreen decked out for Christmas. Blasts of cold air come rushing in as passengers push the great doors open. Vast ceilings. Our footsteps ring out. Leon waits at the ticket counter. The benches are occupied by figures swathed in black, munching on Georgian cheese-bread and warming their hands on cups of coffee purchased from the stand on the other side of the gates that lead to the platforms. A billboard advertises Lake Baikal, its native wildlife, seals, birds, fish. An old man strapped into a wheelchair stares blankly at the image. He clutches the armrests, his hands bare despite the cold, veins bulging. A woman, his wife probably, nudges the wheelchair gently back and forth, as if it were a child's buggy. The man's feet drag along the ground. A teenager, weighed down with luggage, hugs his parents. They cling to him, unable to let him go.

The ceiling is covered wall to wall with a fresco. Vladivostok and Moscow. To one side, the port, with ships, fishermen, the sea tinged with orange. To the other, Red Square, well-dressed women.

The great clock shows the time in Moscow, just like all the other stations all over the country. Back in Europe it's seven hours earlier than here.

I walk over to the windows, gaze out through the glass. Trains. Beyond them, the port. If I travelled by ship to the US, I would arrive in California. To get back to Europe, I'd have to cross all of North America and the Atlantic Ocean. The day after tomorrow I'll be getting on a train to Ulan-Ude, and after that I'll go all the way to Moscow, then Kyiv, Vienna and finally to France. Whichever route I take, I'll have to cross more than one continent. I'm as far away from my destination as it's possible to be.

Leon hands me five tickets, plastic with gold lettering.

'Are you coming?' he says pretending to shiver. 'It's draughty here.'

He holds the door open for me as I hurry towards it.

'I'd like to make a recording of Anna breathing,' I say when we're outside. 'The music doesn't work at all, it's ruining everything. We have to get rid of it.'

He stares at me, dumbfounded.

I start babbling, trying to explain what I mean. We could use a microphone, I don't know if it's technically possible, what I'd like it to do is transmit Anna's breath live while they're doing the number. That would be the soundtrack.

'An act without any music?'

'With her breath for music. Like in the film of *The Diving Bell and the Butterfly*, when all you hear is the sound of the actor breathing. As if the audience is on the inside, in his chest, in his lungs.'

Leon stops and looks at me. Why not, he says. He has a microphone we could attach to her hair, against her skin. We'll have to try it. His lips curl at the corners as if he's trying not to express how pleased he is. He says it could be good. Really good. Suddenly I feel a knot in my stomach. I don't know, I say. We only have one more rehearsal. We're leaving the day after tomorrow.

ANNA IS WAITING for us at the gate.

'It's the cat.'

We follow her to the canteen. Buck is lying sprawled, struggling to breathe.

'He won't survive the night,' she says.

Anton announces from the kitchen, where he is emptying the dishwasher, that he'd like to bury the cat near the bird. Leon thanks him frostily. He'd have appreciated a little help earlier. We won't have enough time, Buck will have to be taken to the dump with the rubbish.

'Leon!' Anna exclaims.

The microphone is switched on. We're experimenting with it, trying to find the best place for it to capture the sound of Anna's breathing. I'll attach it to her forehead, I say. It has to be firmly attached, as close as possible to the body, to block out background sounds. I'll run the wire down her back. I can stitch it to the fabric, weave it into her costume and hide the battery pack in an inside pocket just above the waist. I'll have to undo quite a few of the lights I've sewn in.

This time, I'm the one doing all the work; the only way they can support me is simply by their presence. I work throughout the evening, wrapped in a blanket. Anton plays chess online, headphones clamped to his ears. The others start gathering up their belongings. Towards midnight, Nino heats up some coffee. Anton is asleep in his chair. Anna rouses him and tells him to go to bed. Leon stays on for a while, beside the cat, and then he too goes to bed. Anna sits at my table. She puts on her make-up, tries out different hairstyles, watching tutorials online. By one in the morning, the men have all gone to bed. She leans in over my work, asks me to explain how I've attached the lights. I show her the tube of strong adhesive and all the places where I've rein-forced the stitching. She nods slowly.

Now and again, we check on the cat. He's quiet. I have Anna put on the costume so I can finish stitching it while she is wearing it, with the correct amount of tension. She grimaces as she takes off her clothes. I help her pull the costume over her head. She has goose-bumps. I have her stand with her arms raised, apologise if it's making her arms ache. She shrugs. At long last, it's finished. I turn out the lights. Anna does a twirl. She gives me a worried look:

'How do I look?'

She glows with a softly glinting light, reflected kaleidoscopically in the windows. Her face is made up in midnight blue, her lips, silvery. She looks like a drag-onfly with her long, feathery false eyelashes and waxed, braided hair. I turn on the light in the corridor. She slips out to the bathroom and comes back, her face radiant.

'Thank you, Nathalie.'

While she's changing, I go over to look at the cat. Glassy eyes, slack jaw. I touch him. My heart starts to race. Stone cold. I fold back the cover. His paws are rigid, as if he were standing upright. Liquid has seeped from his ears and rear end. I call Anna. She comes over and kneels beside him, her make-up half removed. She pokes one of his eyes with her finger. Nothing. I stare at her, completely at a loss. Should we wake Leon? She shakes her head, he needs to rest, and besides, what could he do? It's the middle of the night, the rubbish dump doesn't open until eight. We gaze at the cat. The triangular shape of his head is accentuated by the emaciated body. Every rib is visible. I think back to when I arrived, when I first saw him on the stairs, how repellent I found him.

I stroke his nose while Anna folds the paws together.

'What about his eyes?' I ask.

She says you can't close a cat's eyes after they die, their eyelids are controlled by a special muscle.

'Really?'

She says it's common knowledge. Everyone's seen a cat die, their own or someone else's. She hesitates for a moment before asking me to go and fetch some glue. She leans over the cat again, closes one of his eyes with two fingers, runs a thread of glue along the line where the eyelids join. She holds them closed while the glue dries and then does the same for the other eye. She starts talking to me about the horses she watched giving birth when she was a child – sometimes the foal would get stuck, they'd have to cut open the mare to get it out of her belly, to save the mare's life. They usually died.

She wraps the cat in the blanket.

'Sweet little thing,' she murmurs.

She stands up.

'It's time to go to bed,' she says.

DRESS REHEARSAL. The trio warm up. Leon makes some adjustments to the sound system. We all look tired from lack of sleep the night before. We're behind with our programme. Leon took Buck away early in the morning. He had to come back by bus, it took him almost two hours. In the ring, Anna seems wearier than the others. When I asked her at breakfast how she was feeling, she said please not to worry. But I can't help feeling nervous seeing them like this. They seem so sluggish.

I walk over to the audience entrance and have a look around. I haven't been out this way since I arrived six weeks ago. The corridor has been stripped of its posters. In the flickering light I can make out a series of pale patches on the wall where the posters were.

I go back into the ring. Leon adjusts the beam of a projector. He turns it up to maximum brightness. Our eyes meet. I close my eyes. Black dots form beneath my lids, like the marks left by the bird that flew against the glass. The spots persisted even after we'd tried to scrub the glass clean. I think about Igor. I see him in the ring, his image merging with Anna's. Broken, shattered porcelain. I have a flash of Anna leaning over the cat. The bar taken apart. Ulan-Ude. Everything blurs into one. I bow my head, press my fingers to my temples.

'Nathalie? Are you okay?'

Nino is staring at me from the ring. I blink. Nod my head.

'Sure?'

Anna says something to Anton in Russian. Nino comes over and joins me in the seats.

'Anton thinks you need to go outside,' he says gently.

'I'm fine,' I say again. I hear Anton's raised voice.

'I really think you should go outside,' Nino says softly. 'For Anna's sake. You're not in good shape. Anyone can see that.'

I stand up robotically. Leon walks beside me as far as the wings, avoiding my eyes.

I can hear their voices. Nino is arguing with Anton. Anna says something in English, asking them to calm down. No one's been hurt. I don't have to be with them all the time.

Wet snow is falling. Large flakes. I muse about the fact that we've gone from lingering autumn warmth to the first snows of winter. I go back to the caravan, lean against the door, survey the scene. My sewing machine on the little table. The panther costume hanging from the toilet door, the scissors, pins in their metal box. My clothes piled up in the sink along with wrappers from packets of dried fruit.

I start packing my bags. I find the sweets I'd bought to take back as gifts. How pathetic. At my age, I should be bringing back wine, cheese. I wrap the two helmets with their antlers, I want to keep them as souvenirs. I take down the fabrics, remove the pins. I'd used them to mark where I needed to trim. I smile at the idea of customs officers being stabbed when they rummage through my things.

Walking towards the canteen, I hear the sound of Anna's breathing, through the wall. In, out. Loud, amplified a thousand-fold, barely wavering as she comes into contact with the bar. They make adjustments, turn up the volume. The sound grows louder still. Her breath trying to break out of the ring, reach the dome, fill the space with air, make the whole circus float away.

I empty the fridge, wipe down the inside. Then I pick up the aerosol can of whipped cream and open the top. The cream has collapsed and sunk to the bottom, where it sits, quivering slightly. I dump it into the sink where it forms a mound of white. I plunge my finger into the pallid mass and bring it to my lips. Silkiness, crinkled satin, frothy softness. A coating of fat on my tongue. I swallow more than I intended to, lick the mouth of the container. Then I cast it aside and flush the white mound down the sink. It's too late to recycle the tin. Reluctantly I throw it in the bin and unplug everything.

ANTON HAS MADE a reservation in the restaurant of the hotel where I stayed when I first arrived. We're all tired, the tension has been mounting, but Anton insisted. I almost told them I wasn't coming – since they don't seem to want me around anyway. We're underdressed for the occasion. We don't speak. My mushroom soup is delicious, heaped with croutons, as are their Caesar salads. I spoon the soup into my mouth, thinking about a book we read in high school about an elderly woman poisoning her husband with a deadly mushroom soup. A violinist comes over and serenades us. He leans over towards Anna and Nino, whom he must see as a couple in their coordinated outfits – black shirt, white lace. Curtains and carpets dampen the sound. In front of me, there's a picture of a man with the head of a lynx. We eat quickly, before the croutons in my soup have a chance to soak up the liquid and dissolve.

LATER THAT EVENING, I have trouble getting to sleep. Through the caravan window I can see a light flicker on in the corridor inside the circus building. I pull on my coat over my pyjamas. The stage door is open. In the gloom, I can see Nino sitting in the front row of the seats. I walk over and sit down next to him. He's smoking.

'Isn't it no smoking here?'

'Yes.'

The light from backstage barely reaches the ring, fading to darkness at our feet.

'Has Anna gone to bed?' I ask, grasping for something to say.

'Yes.'

'Anton too?'

'How would I know? I don't have to look out for him. I'm not his father – nor his son, for that matter.'

'I'm not trying to attack you.'

'Yeah. Sorry.'

I watch the ripples of smoke from his cigarette. He stubs it out on the metal floor and tucks it into his jacket pocket.

'I'm sorry,' he says again.

'What for?'

'For earlier. When I told you to get out.'

I don't respond.

'Anton's obsessed with safety.'

'I know.'

'He was afraid something would go wrong on the bar. Anna said she was worrying because you hadn't slept all night. She's always been afraid that you feel obliged to stay with us for rehearsals. And then Anton panicked.'

'Is that what she said?'

'Anton doesn't express himself very well. And I'm rubbish at translating.'

I tell him he doesn't need to keep apologising. I'm just sorry I've never really managed to communicate with Anton.

'He's not even aware of the fact that I speak for him,' Nino continues.

'He's lucky to have you.'

Nino shrugs.

'He never stops telling me that I have to find a new partner.'

'What do you think about that?'

'One way or the other, he'll never forgive me. Ever.'

'But if that's what he's asking you to do . . .'

'No,' Nino says, interrupting me. 'It's because I was trying to catch Igor.'

I try to make sense of this. Then he says:

'When I saw that we weren't going to catch him with the bar I dropped everything. I ran over to try and stop his fall with my body. Anton was rooted to the spot.'

I try and picture the scene.

'He's been involved in a few accidents,' Nino says. 'Some of them he's caught. Some people. I don't know what happened this time. He probably couldn't quite take in what was happening.'

I ask if it would have made any difference. What does he know, he replies. His own injuries were bad enough – broken ribs, both wrists. Igor fell from a height of seven metres. He broke his neck. It was a miracle he survived.

'You probably saved his life.'

'I've told you, I don't know.'

I take a deep breath.

The minutes tick by.

I ask him if he's noticed that the smell isn't so strong, the animal smell. Not since the heating's been turned off. He says he doesn't know what we're all talking about, he's never smelt it at all. I feel for his hand, trying to grasp it. He pulls away, puts his arm round my shoulder.

'Are you ready, the three of you?'

'Don't worry.'

PART III

ANNA AND I have a second-class sleeper for four. The others are in third class, where the carriages aren't divided into compartments and there is space to lay the bar down on the ground and keep an eye on it. We've just crossed the Amur river. Snow has begun to fall. I take the top bunk. I put my things in the mesh pouch on the wall above my couchette, make up my bed and then climb back down to join Anna at the window. Snow covers the rails. The horizon is no longer visible. The rumbling of the train barely stirs the deepening silence. Black spots appear before my eyes again. I see what I think are marmots and then remember that they're probably hibernating. My eyes are dazzled from the blinding snow, but it's just my own blood I'm seeing.

We go to get water for tea from the samovar at one end of the carriage and meet up with the others. We follow them to their carriage where they are surrounded by a group of soldiers curious about this strange piece of luggage stretched out beneath several bunks. They joke around with us, teasing us about this giant corpse – how far are we going to have to travel to make it disappear? The train stops at stations where all the signs are covered in ice. Places that barely have names. Anton buys dried fish from the women on the platforms. The stops are brief, the sales take place through the window. We lean out with money, the fish are thrown up to us, we catch them in the air, clutching them tightly, as if they were still alive.

'This is omoul,' Anton tells me, unravelling a piece of netting. 'Of Baikal. Try it!'

He talks to us about Irkutsk, tells us legends of Baikal, of shamans. The soldiers join us with chocolate, we laugh and joke. The compartment is heavy with smells of fish, instant coffee, bodies. Conversation dwindles.

Soon, we have nothing more to say. We sit there, lined up on the bench seats.

We are two days and nights away from Ulan-Ude. I try to give shape to this span of time. I watch Anton chewing on fish. I picture the man I saw panicking in the patisserie when faced with all those different cakes. I can't reconcile the two. In a bag at his feet, the bird boxes.

Late that afternoon more soldiers join the convoy. Anna and I are sitting in their seats. We go back to our compartment. A woman walks down the corridor towards the toilets carrying her child's chamber pot.

'I think the recruits like you,' I say to Anna.

'Whatever.'

Her cheeks are pink and flushed.

A couple occupy the bunks opposite ours. The woman is dressed in tight-fitting purple polyester, her T-shirt rolled up above her midriff. Their skin looks dry and mottled. I have an image of the seals in the posters at the station at Vladivostok. She takes some bed linen out of their bags, books of crosswords, a large bowl of jellied meat. Anna starts chatting to them. I can hear them from my couchette. She tells me later that they're going to meet their daughter in Yekaterinburg, five days away by train.

The man walks off down the corridor in his socks, carrying his toilet bag. His wife follows him with two cups. Anna spreads cream on her face. I see her taking a pill before she gets into bed. The couple come back. The woman pours boiling water over the meat. Steam clouds the window. Cloying smells drift upwards. Chewing sounds. I suck on a Sugarsea sweet to try and block it all out. Anna sleeps soundly.

THE WOMAN TALKS in her sleep. She keeps me awake. I go to the toilets. Deserted corridor. I look haggard. I splash water on my face. The water drains slowly away. It sits in the bottom of the basin and leaves a halo of murky white. I feel vaguely nauseous. I don't know if it is from the sweets or the swaying of the train. I open the curtains over a window in the corridor. The sky scrolls by. Stars. Siberian night. Cold. Freezing everything but the train. Unseeable. Back in my bunk, I toss and turn. I feel scorched by contact with the mattress. I haven't paid attention to the raw patch on my neck for a week. The jellied meat is still sitting out on the table, fat congealing on its surface. When the woman dug into it with her spoon, the grating sound of the spoon against the plate made me want to reach out and touch it. Would the pâté feel warm or cool, grainy or gelatinous? Would my finger slide in easily? How many different textures do we touch in one lifetime? Is it possible to keep track of them all?

Had my father done the wrong thing in giving me that sleeping pill? I've always thought of him as my protector. He held my hand whenever we walked along the road until I was well into my teens, it was embarrassing, people thought I was his girlfriend. The last time we saw each other, he seemed smaller. Stooped. I wanted to cry out to him and say that we too would both become particles one day.

THE NEXT DAY, the landscape has turned to wasteland. We pass disused factories, cranes swaying precariously. Water towers for ghost cities. Aircraft marooned on the steppe as if waiting for fuel. No sign of any human beings except for maintenance workers along the railway lines. Construction workers in their yellow helmets and gloves, scarves wrapped around their mouths to protect against dust. We follow the shoreline of a lake. At the bend, I press my face to the window as the back of the train comes into view for the first time from my compartment.

At Khabarovsk, Anna and I meet up with the other three on the platform. We buy drinks from the vending machines, a choice of two brands: Coca-Cola or something Russian. I keep an eye on the others. The train could leave without us.

As I undress for the second night, Anna glances at the psoriasis on the back of my neck.

'It's spreading,' she says.

I mutter something about buying some ointment when I get home. She shakes her head. Hadn't she already said I could use hers? She rummages in her toilet bag, takes out a jar of moisturiser and tells me to stand in front of her. I do as she says. I hand her a wipe but she thrusts it back at me.

'Don't be such a pain,' she says as she spreads the lotion on with her fingers. 'Is it serious?'

I shake my head. It happens when I'm stressed out. She puts the lid back on the jar.

'That's good.'

ULAN-UDE. We've arrived. The passengers haul themselves from the train. Vast staircases lead from the platforms to the station concourse. No escalators. We climb
slowly, absorbed into the crowd. Shawls, furs, laboured
breathing, backpacks, suitcases being dragged over the
frozen ground. An inflatable elephant points the way
to the bus for the festival a few kilometres outside the
city. I haven't slept enough. I glance absently out of the
window. Central square and city hall. Walls glistening
in the morning sunshine. We pass a giant concrete bust
of Lenin, bigger than the bus. Then down a busy main
street that leads out to the steppes.

The road runs beside a river. Anton, sitting next to me, points at it and says:

'Selenga river. You can follow it to my village.'

Before long, a colourful patchwork of caravans and tents comes into view out on the plain.

Technicians scurrying back and forth. Frenetic activity. Intense concentration. A hubbub of indistinct sounds. As soon as we step off the bus I become aware of how famous Anton and Nino are. Other artists greet them, embrace them, people approach them to ask for autographs, photographs with them. A group of children cluster around Anton. He lifts them with one hand, balancing them one by one on his open palm. Nino urges him to hurry, they have to go to the artists' registration under the big top at the other end of the site. As we walk, I watch him sizing up the equipment, talking with Anton; he tells him he's going to a particular tent to find out about his parents, comments on a new development in lighting. Anna keeps her eyes fixed on the crowd of spectators beyond the barriers. Faces of Siberian peoples, some paler than others. Athletes in their winter coats distinguishable from spectators only by their make-up and headdress, striking portraits. A parade of horses being led at a trot, fleece blankets on their backs, frozen whiskers.

Anton and Nino go to register while I wait outside with Leon and Anna. Anna buys burgers for us from a food truck. A drunk leans over to whisper in her ear. Leon puts his arm round her waist. She makes a show of being irritated, says the man was harmless enough.

'I've had a look at the programme,' Nino says as we are eating in the artists' warm-up area. 'There's no general parade here. We do our act, nothing else. We're on second, just after the tightrope walker. He uses smoke in his act, which is a bit annoying as it could make it harder for us to see. But by the time they've dismantled the high wire it should have gone away. We have our technical rehearsal at four. And right now, Anton and I have an interview with a local journalist.'

We agree to meet up in the ring for the technical rehearsal. Nino gives me a box with a set of earphones attached, in case I want to listen to the live translation of the commentary.

I've never seen such feverish activity backstage. People milling about, costumes in protective plastic coverings, make-up cases, hair products. Anna and I look for a spot at one of the tables. Each one has a large mirror framed by lightbulbs. The noise from hairdryers and ventilation pipes is constant.

'I'll go and change into my costume,' Anna says hesitantly.

While she's gone, I go and look at the ring through a gap in the tent. Scenery with a marine theme. A mermaid hangs from the ceiling, wrapped in seaweed made from ribbons. Beneath her, a man in a snake costume writhes on a carpet made to look like sand and rock.

I don't put the full make-up on Anna. Just enough to give us an idea of the effect it creates in this ring which is so much larger than the one in Vladivostok. I'll touch it up before their performance this evening.

Anna can't tear herself away from her phone. I have to ask her to look up, I can't work on her expression with her looking down. She explains that it's her father. He's here, he wants to know when he can see her. She shuts the phone down. She'll get back to him after the show. She needs to stay focussed.

The marine-themed scenery has been replaced by a black carpet, the spotlights adjusted for the dim lighting required for our act. Anna is glowing in her bodysuit of lights, sparks flying off her. We can just see Anton and Leon in shadow, leaning against a pillar, Nino seated on the bar, which is still encased in its protective wrapping.

They're not in costume.

'We can't use the microphone,' Nino announces.

I try to determine if he's being serious.

'It's to do with frequencies,' Leon explains. 'Ours isn't compatible with the festival's system.'

Anna gazes up at the technical equipment. The movement of her head makes Anton's face glimmer beside her.

'An event at this level,' she says. 'Surely there must be a solution?'

Leon shakes his head. That's just it. He's been talking with someone in charge. 'Almost all the frequencies are taken up by all the international radio and television stations. We can't use our mic because of the risk of interference. It's obvious, we should have thought about it before, we should have warned the organisers, let them know in advance.'

I remind him that we only decided to do it just before we left Vladivostok.

'Yeah, but all the same!' he says, seething.

I try and think fast. The microphone idea was mine, I thought of it at the last minute. Why don't they simply use the music they were originally planning to use? As if I'd never said anything?

'Absolutely not!' Anton objects.

'Why not?' Anna and I ask in unison.

'Security.'

You can't change an act just like that, he says, it's not safe. It's bad luck.

No one speaks.

Anton says they'll come back the following year. They'll be even better. With five triples.

Anna hugs her arms to her chest. She walks over to the seats. Her blue make-up prevents me from seeing her expression.

The technicians up in the rigging lean down towards us, as if to ask why we're debating instead of rehearsing.

'Have you seen the crowd coming this evening?' Anna asks softly from the other side of the ring.

I look over at the others. Surely they aren't going to back out now. Not now that they're ready!

'*We're* ready,' Nino says tilting his chin bitterly towards the rigging. 'But they're not.'

Anna turns round, her eyes shining.

'Can we at least make an appearance?'

'Make an appearance?' Leon mouths.

'We come out and wave at the audience. And leave. In our leopard costumes.'

She asks me if I brought them, with the helmets, the antlers, everything. I nod.

'That's ridiculous,' Nino says.

'There's nothing wrong with them,' Anna retorts. 'They're fine.'

'I mean coming out and waving.'

'That's all we did for that week in Vladivostok.'

'That was different.'

Anna turns to Anton and says:

'I have no way of knowing what's going to happen between now and next year.'

She stares at him. Anton holds her gaze, then turns to look at Nino, who hasn't stopped staring at the bar and telling Anna not to say such things.

In the end Anton agrees. They won't do their act this evening, they'll just go round the ring once waving at the audience. A mark of respect for tradition.

Another silence. Anna says it will give them a chance to wear them, the first costumes I made for them.

All four of them look at me. I want to disappear.

Nino nods slowly.

'There's still the problem of the music,' Leon points out.

Anton takes his phone from his pocket. He wants us to listen to something. The speaker isn't working. He turns the volume up to maximum. We lean in close. I recognise the tune, *My Way*. In Russian, syrupy, very slow. Anna wrinkles her nose:

'What's that?'

'He's been listening to that before we perform ever since I've known him,' Nino says.

'Seriously?' I ask.

'I like this song,' Anton says.

Anna laughs. They're going to parade round the ring to that? What does Leon think of it? He opens his arms wide, gives a forced laugh, says he's never choreographed anything to that. A couple walk in wearing skin-coloured body suits. It's time for us to vacate the ring.

'Seriously,' I say again. 'What are you actually going to do?'

As we leave, it's decided. They'll keep the suit of lights and the microphone for the next big occasion. This time, they'll wear the leopard and forest costumes.

They'll come on without the bar, to the version of *My Way* Anton's chosen. The festival will be able to play it from a computer easily. They'll join hands in the centre of the ring, fan out in different directions and walk round the ring once in front of the audience. They'll meet up again in the middle and come back together backstage.

ANNA SITS DOWN in front of the mirror. She wipes the colour from her lips, grimaces to relax her features. I prepare a new palette. She stops me. She doesn't want any make-up. She'd rather appear without it. Just this once.

'Are you sure?'

'Yes.'

I fix her hair for her while she removes her make-up. A tight bun. I attach the headband with the panther ears. When I've finished, she quickly checks her phone. We catch each other's eyes in the mirror.

'You're beautiful,' I say.

She stands up, places one hand on her waist, says she doesn't need to be beautiful.

At the main entrance, the crowd continues to swell, packing in ever more tightly. As I walk over towards the seats Leon grabs me by the hand and leads me outside. He loops a wire round my neck, like the one the technicians have. He carries on walking, explaining that he's met an old associate, he's arranged it all. We go back into the tent through a service entrance at the back of the ring. We follow the safety lights, Leon still holding my hand. At the foot of one of the towers, we stop.

'Up you go,' he whispers behind me.

He places my hands on the rungs and follows close behind me. I try not to think about the ever-receding ground. We climb to a platform at a height of about ten metres, where a man is waiting for us. He gives us a harness, tells me to put it on and attaches it to the tower with a carabiner. He checks all the fastenings, tightens the harness at my waist. My vertigo intensifies when I realise that we are standing on the platform the tightrope walker's cable is attached to. All the seats are full. From up here the audience look tiny. Leon crouches behind me, one hand on my stomach. His body has had no contact with mine since we began to climb. The technician signals to the tightrope walker who I can now see on the tower opposite. He's dressed in white. Wide trousers.

He steps closer to the void. The house lights dim, a spot-light shines on the wire. The violins grow louder. I click the on switch on my commentary translation pack. A male voice, uncertain. I remove my headset.

'Something wrong?' Leon says.

'It's his Russian accent, it's too strong, I can't under-stand a word.'

The audience vanishes in a cloud of smoke. I picture our trio, waiting behind the curtains. The smoke clears. I cling tightly to Leon. He presses his hand harder against my stomach. Over on the other side of the wire, the tight-rope artist has stepped out and begun to walk.

When we parted ways on the station platform the day after the festival, we promised we'd see each other again. In the end, we never did. The following year, they won a major competition. We stayed in touch at first, on the internet. But you know how it is when you live so far apart, things fade of their own accord. And I never had an address for them. They were always on the move. Do you know, I never even knew their surnames. For me, they'll always be Anna, Leon, Anton and Nino. I don't know what became of them. Whether or not they carried on. I read that Anton, who was much older, had died. I don't know why I'm telling you this.

I've had an idea. I know you feel claustrophobic when you're here in Switzerland. But would you not like to at least come back to Europe? Now that you have more time, we could see each other more often. I don't like thinking of you all alone over there. We could find you somewhere where you could feel at home. We have open spaces here too, plains. In Spain, Belgium or France for example. Think about it. We're here, waiting for you. Just give me a sign and I'll be waiting for you on the platform.

Look after yourself.

Nathalie

PS Thousands of birds flew into the square earlier this evening. They flutter around the people gathering outside the circus tent.

Tonight is the opening night. There are birds perched everywhere, on the power lines, the guy ropes, the strings of lights that festoon the tent. Like unlit light bulbs. Did you know there's a species of bird with wings so bulky they can't launch themselves from the ground? They end up staying in the air. They can spend their whole lives without ever landing. They sleep on the wing, ten kilometres above our heads.

You know, when I think of all those little bodies suspended between earth and sky, it makes me smile to remind myself that for some of them, their first flight begins with a fall.

DAUNT BOOKS

Founded in 2010, Daunt Books Publishing grew out of Daunt Books, independent booksellers with shops in London and the south of England. We publish the finest writing in English and in translation, from literary fiction – novels and short stories – to narrative non-fiction, including essays and memoirs. Our modern classics list revives authors whose work has unjustly fallen out of print. In 2020 we launched Daunt Books Originals, an imprint for bold and inventive new writing.

www.dauntbookspublishing.co.uk